FOR
BID
DEN
VOICE

ONDER DELIGOZ

This novel is entirely a work of fiction. The names, characters and incidents portrayed in it are the work of the author's imagination. Any resemblance to actual persons, living or dead, events or locations is entirely coincidental.

ISBN 978-1-7380243-0-8

Crane Books
www.cranebooks.ca

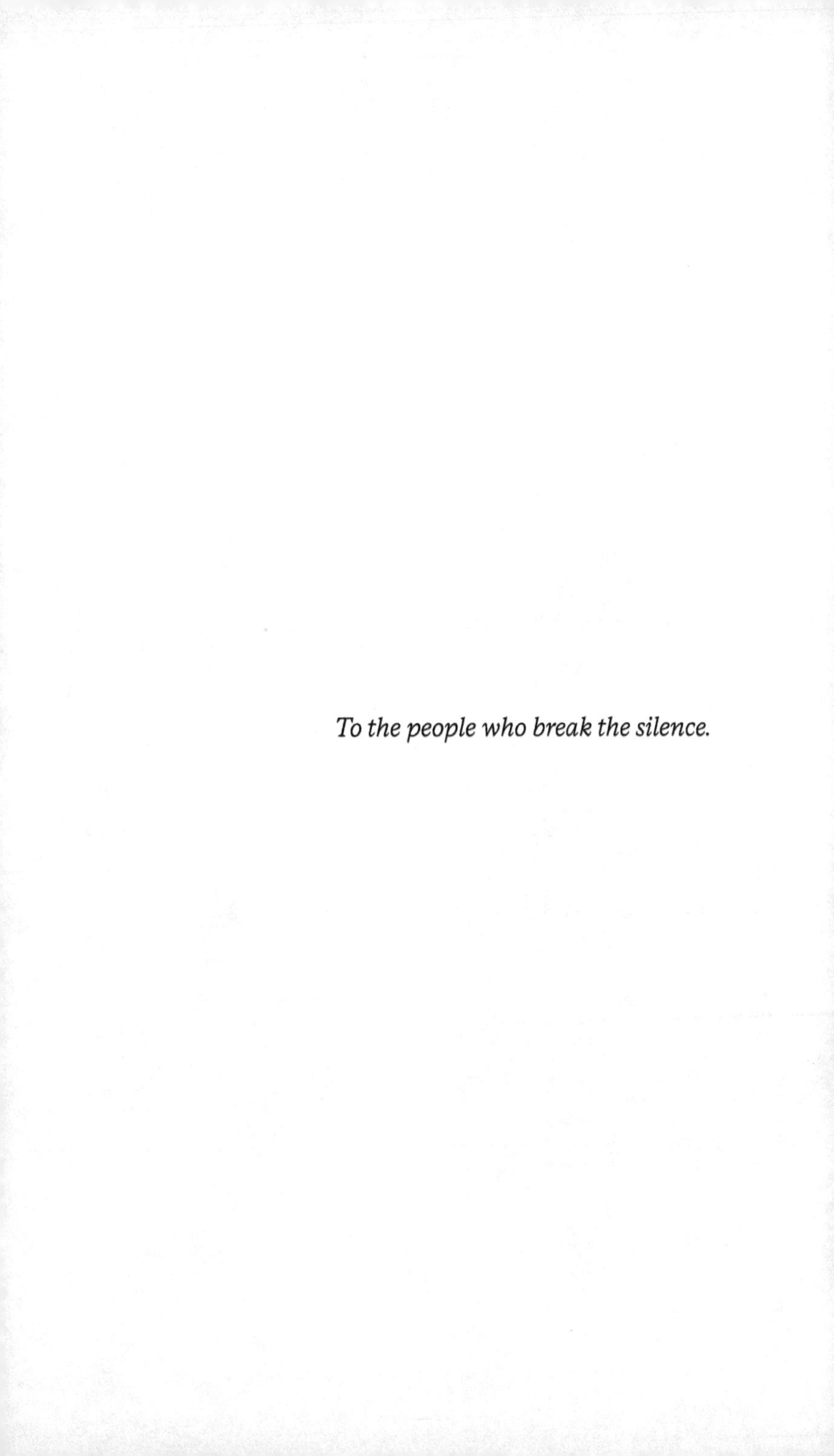

To the people who break the silence.

CONTENTS

From: Yusuf
Subject: ***Please give this woman's voice back to her***
August 19th, 2014

I **wonder if there's any other pickle shop** in the world that opens at six in the morning? I'm quite sure there isn't. I mean, I was sitting there squirting foamy glass cleaner and sparkling up the display windows with some bunched-up newspaper while everyone in this huge city of Istanbul slept soundly in their beds. In a little while, I was going to go inside to wipe the dust off the pickle jars, inwardly swearing a whopping mouthful at the pickle maker Hayri as I went. I mean, I was going bonkers from sleeplessness as I muttered to the pickled cabbage, and I wanted nothing more than to light into Hayri, who was snoozing away in his leather armchair in the corner, crumpled up in a ball. At noon, Pickleman Hayri would go to the mosque for prayers, and maybe I could take a seat on the wooden stool in the corner and get a little shut-eye... That, my friends, was as great an expectation as I had in this life. Not much to ask for, just a tiny bit of shut-eye on a wooden stool, and the little bit of calm that came with it. How was I to know that I was about to see something that would leave me sleepless for so many days that my present state would seem like a dream?

I was trying to catch a sliver of yesterday's sports scores in the newspaper as I wiped the last of the glass when the old man popped out of nowhere and grabbed my arm. *"What happened?"* I yelled. I would have fallen onto the pavement if he wasn't holding my arm as if it were a roll of cash. *"What do you want?"* He didn't reply, and just dragged me inside. I was flopping around in his grasp like a minnow on a line. He hauled me toward the table with the computer and register. This wasn't a good sign. Hayri had forbidden me from getting anywhere near that table. In fact, on the day I started work, his very first words to me -he had not even said *"hello"*- were, *"Don't think about touching the register or table and ruining the shop's positive vibes."* That's when I understood money was quite dear to him. Great. So, why had he dragged me over to that precious register? I wondered, was he going to claim that the cash in the register -which he counted so often it was as if he thought it was going to multiply the more he flicked it through his- was missing and say I stole it? I wouldn't have done such a thing. I'm sure the asshole had miscounted.

Hayri pointed at his computer screen and said, *"Hey, check it out, see how the infidel gets snuffed out."* Slowly, I understood the matter had nothing to do with money, though probably I was in shock because my eyes remained stuck on the register. I would've preferred to have my arm pop out of its socket rather than be accused of theft by a money-hungry bastard like Pickleman Hayri. *"Heaven is for those who die hungry to do whatever necessary is for their honor, not for those who steal,"* my father had admonished me, and that was the golden earring that swung from my ear. I would've made my father the King of the Road if he hadn't forced me to work next to this maniac; of course, that was another matter entirely. I actually did not have the right to be mad at my father. It was my very own decision to work to make my own school allowance. And my father found me a job next to this *dangalak*.

From the very first day that I met Hayri, I called him *dangalak*, as he fully fit the meaning of it; he was thoughtless and irrational. When I was in high school, I only worked for *dangalak* Hayri during breaks. High school was over and despite the rudeness of Hayri, I was going to have to be patient and work full time for him. This was because, when my father passed away, I did not want my mother to have to work more to make money for my university prep school expenses. But my goodwill was constantly abused by dangalak Hayri's terribleness.

I relaxed a bit mentally, but I was grimacing in pain. My arm was still in Hayri's grasp. He sat down in his leather armchair, which made crumpling noises as he yanked me hard toward him. *"Lookie here, I hope you learn a lesson, check out how the blond infidel pleads for his life!"* And I totally went limp. *"Who's the blond infidel, who's he pleading to, why's he begging for his life?"* I said. Hayri clicked the mouse and at that moment, I lost all faith in the good of the world.

Someone like Pickleman Hayri, who had neglected to add a moustache to his long beard, held a blond-haired guy kneeling in front of him by the scruff of the neck with one hand, and brandished a knife in the other. He wore dark-blue plastic flip-flops on his bare feet. He swung the knife in his right hand as spittle spewed from his maniacal mouth onto the monitor. The cameraman, who was most likely a scruffy guy like him, kept zooming in once in a while, I guess to better reflect the horror of the moment. If only he didn't do that, I might have been less nauseous. Spittle that accumulated in the lip recesses of a guy shouting *"Allah is great!"* after every sentence was disgusting enough. Hearing Allah's name uttered in vain by such a foul mouth made it all the more repulsive.

I've always hated those who rally around the phrase *"Allahu Akbar- Allah is great-"* and unfortunately, my neighborhood was too full of men like this. I get pissed off to the point of smacking walls whenever I hear the name of the Creator — to whom I'm grateful for creating my mother — from these filthy mouths and grieve to the point of crying. I felt the same way at that moment. But this time, I was in no condition to slam my fist into the wall, let alone cry. First, I needed to break free from Pickleman Hayri's vise-like grip. Meanwhile, my eyes were peeled to the video, as I wondered what was going to happen. The blond guy was saying stuff in a language I didn't understand. Of course, in a voice comparatively weaker than that of the bearded guy who was flinging a knife over his head, and with a face crumpled in agony.

Finally, the bearded guy looked into the camera with hatred-filled eyes, shrieked at the top of his lungs, thrust his knife into the air -at this point, I promptly forgot the pain in my arm- and slit the throat of the blonde man in a single motion. While the blood of the blonde guy spurted onto the parched ground, mine seemed to freeze. *"Man, did you see that!"* Hayri said proudly. *"I'm telling you; this is jihad. It's necessary to murder infidels. May Allah give this freedom fighters strength. They are taking the vengeance of the ummah."*

I opened my eyes and looked at this *dangalak*. He was like a grotesque vampire sucking blood from his victim's neck. So, it looked like the freak of nature had been watching these videos for days, his tongue hanging out of his mouth. Panting like a dog, he'd been having orgasms while watching that guy's head being lopped off. I wanted to scream, *"What ummah, what vengeance, you son-of-a-bitch!"* Naturally, I was scared. Despite my shock, I didn't want to get smacked by Hayri, who probably would have started licking infidel blood off the dusty floor had he had the honour of hosting the execution in his shop. Once psychopaths start smacking you, they don't stop until there's nothing of you left.

What could you expect from a man who never read anything to understand about humanity? And to think the Allahless bitch shouted, *"Allahu Akbar!"* Beardy had always been a fanatic who wore religious cloaks, never uttered a single word to his female customers, and locked up his wife at home. But to be honest with you, I didn't expect this. Then again, I should have kept in my mind the day I left a water pan in front of the door for stray dogs or cats to slake their thirst. He rebuked me sharply as he poured the water out. His excuse was that animals would cause an infestation in the shop. Damn, you'd have thought this was a butcher shop. You're a pickleman, for Allah's sake, a pickleman! Dumbass thought the water bowl would give dogs ideas and they'd saunter into the shop and wolf down a barrel of pickled cucumbers.

But I should have known that *dangalak* Hayri would go insane in a whole new way after he met horse-head Mahmut at one of those gatherings where the bearded ones hold hands and go into a trance by jumping up and down and headbanging while they slap their tambourines. (They call him horse-head because, well, he's got a head like a horse's - his chin is in a different postal code from his eyes.) I've seen the videos of those gatherings — they even have one where three guys in the front cab of a semi-rig hop up and down like madmen when maybe they should be paying attention to the highway. A disco ball spinning eternally over their heads was the only thing missing.

Since then, there hadn't been a day in two months that horse-head Mahmut hadn't dropped by the shop. He and Hayri spend at least an hour on the computer every day, whispering some stuff to each other close enough for their beards to touch. They'd get carried away once in a while, saying *"mashallah, elhamdulillah."* I assumed that they were watching one of those shows where the believers want you to see that Islam is modern, so they fill the stage with *kittens* comprised of nothing but pumped-up boobs, asses and lips, who clap to belly-dance music. *Dangalak* Hayri, of course, did not approve of this intriguing concept. But being part of a fanclub of a concept one doesn't approve of is one of the classic dilemmas of our land. Where else is the proverb *"Do what the imam says, not what he does"* passed down from generation to generation? I mean, these are the lands where those men who stone women over adultery accusations in the morning make love to the same women at night. These two bums having orgasms at the computer were just a microcosm of the weird order that exist in our country.

Eventually, I realized they were probably not watching the *kitten* show because they kept adding *"mujahideen," "murder is obligatory,"* and *"die infidels"* to all their *"Allah bless"*-ing. The whispering conversations turned into rally sessions pumping each other up with slogans like *"We set up an Islamic state, the conquest is ours."* Horse-head started bringing books and magazines for our *dangalak* Hayri to read. He explained which news websites Hayri needed to follow. Captivated Hayri was doing whatever horse-head told him. Of course, he was on the orders of the head of the religious group, to whom horse-head was the right hand. The rest of the fanatics had started satisfying their pickle needs only at Hayri's shop. As I worked in the shop, I couldn't understand what he was watching all the time, as he wore earphones. As if hopping and jumping around practically every night isn't enough, I thought, the psychopath is watching tambourine trance videos. In fact, dancing with the tambourine wasn't enough, the psychopath was dancing with blood.

Their proliferation like rabbits, that can become pregnant within minutes after one-month pregnancy, was another nightmare entirely. They suddenly showed up everywhere with their weird outfits and behaviour. In fact, a segment had come out of their weird outfits only to enter expensive suits, luxury cars and luxury homes referred to as 'palaces.' Turning into loyal clients of the group's members has made them rich. Of course, they all had the same mindset.

The noon call to prayer saved me. Hayri shut down his computer the moment he heard it, locked the register, and passed by me to step outside as though nothing had happened. I gawked at his back. Would he really lay prone in front of Allah as if he was not wild with the blood of that miserable sap on the screen a little while before? Yes! Since he had an Allah who rewarded the spilling of the blood of infidels, he would prostrate himself with great faith and appetite. That was definitely not my Allah. My Allah was the Allah who created my mother.

No sooner did psychopath Hayri leave the shop than I ran to the bathroom behind the cabinet. I stuck my head under the faucet. I was looking at the sink drain without blinking my eyes. It was as if blood rather than water poured down my head. I was afraid of losing my mind. All of us in these lands are potential victims, and no one could guarantee me that a knife wouldn't be plunged into my throat one day. Bloodshot eyes were staring back at me when I looked in the mirror. *"Hey, get a grip, man!"*

No matter how much I tried to mollify myself, my limbs continued to shake. How was I supposed to rid myself of the blood that had flooded my face? I have never tried, but getting drunk or smoking a spliff could've saved me. I stepped outside to get some fresh air. I stood in front of the door. Every person who walked by had a slit throat. Why had this video made me as scared as a three-year old kid, as if I'd never watched films that showed heads and limbs cut off like tree branches?

"Allah damn you, Hayri!" I shouted at the street. The people walking by looked at me strangely, even though they were the ones with bloody throats. *"I'll spit right in the middle of your face that had the orgasm while the guy's throat was being slit."* Just then, a vision of Pickleman Hayri's face manifested itself, and, seeing the perversion in his eyes, I understood the answer I'd been searching for. Given half the chance, he would've cut off my head and screamed for bloody jihad, too. Who knows, I might very well have been his first target. As it was, I was living like an infidel, chatting up my girlfriends on the phone, wearing tight-fitting

trousers and not letting my beard grow out.

I was dreading the old pervert's return from prayers, but maybe he was right and Allah exists, because there was no trace of him all afternoon. He had probably gotten another migraine, and gone home and keeled over. I waited for his wife to call me and say, in her best attempt to sound hoarse, *"Esselamu alaikum, Hayri is not feeling well, he won't be coming."* The pathetic dangalak, as if it was not enough to steal the sun away from the poor housebound woman -she could not go outside without his permission- he had also seized her voice. Whenever the wretched woman spoke to another man, she had to try to sound like a man because it was not halal -meaning it is not approved by Allah- for a woman to speak to a man she wasn't married to. *"Someone will hear your fire of hell voice!"* he had yelled at her when she had called him at the shop the other day. *"What if someone else picked up the phone!"* How could a person's voice be compared to the fire of hell? How could a person's voice be forbidden? Of course, I wasn't surprised by this psychotic bout of Hayri's. However, I was really sad for the poor woman, whom I hadn't seen before and, most likely, would not in the future.

And that's exactly what happened. Once I heard the ringing I went inside unwillingly. I wanted to stay as far from the table as possible because that table was not different from a hangman's gallows to me. I stopped two steps behind the table and reached for the phone. On the other end, I heard the hoarse voice.

_Assalamu alaikum, Hayri is not feeling well, he won't be coming, he wants you to close up the shop.
_Yes ma'am.

She was about to hang up when I blurted out: Ma'am, wait

a minute, ma'am… May Allah protect you from tyrants. I could tell that she became petrified on the other end of the receiver. Instead of wishing her husband a speedy recovery, I had wished for Allah to protect her. Perhaps she appreciated that someone besides herself was aware she needed protection. But she only took a deep breath and hung up the phone. Listening to the dial tone, I completed the prayer I couldn't finish on the phone because I couldn't openly say that I didn't want the poor woman to suffer any longer. *"Oh God, please give this woman's voice back to her,"* I said. *"I know it is impossible to give her life back, but at least give this imprisoned woman back her voice."* Just then, I heard:

_Assalamu alaikum
I looked up.
_Welcome, Uncle Selami, c'mon in.
_First take the greetings of Allah.
_I already said, "Welcome, Uncle Selami!
_You should say, *"Waalaikum selam,"* not *"Welcome,"* *"Waalaikum salam!"* Is it so difficult to receive a greeting, to show respect by kissing my hand, to say *"C'mon in hadji."*

Dangalak Hayri's customers were as psychotic as him. Selami, a chicken-shop owner, was one of these guys who thought putting on a cloak and growing out his beard made him an Islamic scholar worthy of having his hand kissed. And if I kissed his hand that day, he was going to have me kiss his cloak a day later. I would never even have said hello to him if I didn't work there. As everybody in the neighborhood knew, this sixty-five year-old guy had tried to marry a little refugee Syrian girl even though he was already married. This is not legal in our country, but men like Selami make their own law and girls from poor families in the east have to obey it. He'd been so hungry for the young flesh that he'd never noticed that it had all been a swindle.

He went to Kilis, a city is full of Syrian refugees, to get married with a fourteen year old girl. After a video call with the girl, he paid two swindlers 20,000 lira and 50,000 lira worth gold as they agreed in Istanbul. Once he handed over the money and gold, the swindlers run away from the place they met as fast as Ussain Bolt. Of course he couldn't report the swindlers to the police. He turned back Istanbul with nothing but a red face. Everyone in this neighborhood understood that the girl was part of the scheme and laughed out loud when a red-faced Selami returned to explain what had happened to him. This was a classic case of hunters being hunted, and I was pleased to extend my congratulations to the swindlers for making Selami return home empty-handed. I swear, this was a type of con artist I could appreciate. I didn't have any problem whatsoever with them taking money off of old fucks that wandered around with their dicks in their hands. In fact, they conducted a sort of service to humanity. Those swindlers were better off spending that money on a couple of glasses of booze instead of having some poor girl cry in the clutches of an old bastard like Selami. Cheers!

I could not go so low as to show a modicum of respect to Selami, who went on with his life without the slightest bit of shame on his face, as if it wasn't him who went in hot pursuit of a little girl only to be swindled. He saw that I cared nothing for what he said and changed his mind about buying some pickles. He exited the shop, mumbling *"Oh, for Allah's sake."* I followed him out the shop, locked the door, and headed out into the streets. As I was walking,

I thought about the neighbourhood that I grew up in. I am eighteen years old, but still feel like a foreigner here. This is a neighbourhood mostly inhabited by conservative people. It is a neighbourhood where even the alcoholics or drug dealers who blackout with the cheapest of drugs, compete for conservativeness. Of course I, too, was affected by this atmosphere. I learned both how to pray and to swear from the elderly in this neighborhood. But this was my limit. I did not judge anyone because of the lifestyle that they chose. Even if I was right, I never got in a quarrel with anyone. If I was too angry or sad, all I did was swear.

I can't remember how many hours I wandered in the utter darkness. My body was still icy cold. I was sure I wasn't going to eat for days. As someone who can't even endure watching a knife rubbing along the throat of a sacrificial sheep, I saw a head that was swinging in the hands of a humanoid monster. What did I do to deserve this? What could a man have done to deserve to have his head cut off in such a vicious manner? How could permission have been granted to split into pieces a servant that had been created by Allah? Why couldn't Allah who had created my mother have intervened in this monstrosity? The Creator needed to ensure I found a logical answer to this question in a hurry. Otherwise, the way things looked, He was at risk of losing a believer. While even children put their dolls to rest in their embrace, how was it He didn't defend a servant he'd created? Why didn't He own up to his incredible work?

While these questions were buzzing around in my head, I realized I had come full circle to end up in front of the shop again. I was like a sacrificial cow that had freed itself from the clutches of the butcher, only to return to the slaughtering grounds after running rampant through the streets. There was another woman walking along the empty avenue at this hour of the night! Giving her a glance, she was a tourist as far as could tell in the dark. I gave her the once over as she passed by me. I was sure I annoyed her, but I couldn't defeat my curiosity. That's the moment when that indelibly etched idiom, *"Curiosity got the better of me"* became a reality. We came eye-to-eye as she passed next to me. She had tattoos on the side of her eyes. I stared at her face to discern the shape of tattoos, but I couldn't see due to the darkness. She smiled the moment we made eye contact, then she moved on. I couldn't figure out if her smile was a defense mechanism or if it was a sign of friendliness, I contemplated pursuing the matter by going after her and asking, but I just diddn't up to it. My day was ruined, no thanks to the *dangalak* Hayri. There was no way I was going to ruin my night by being labeled a molester. I should be heading home and hitting the sack while I still had my wits about me.

From: Hifza
Subject: ***I know better now how this fear causes people to become slaves***
August 22nd, 2014

I **had never seen so many air conditioners** in my life. As a young girl who grew up with drafty windows and a stove that never completely heated our home, I knew quite well what wintry cold was. However, the little apparatus hanging on the wall, which turned the hellish heat of a huge building into winter, really amazed me. All around me, red numbers flashed over ticket booths as dozens of people bustled to get their identity cards, but I was staring at the air-conditioning unit in front of me as if it were a television.

It was like the first time I saw a banana. I was so little I couldn't even reach the door handle yet. It's as if that bunch of bananas in the transparent bag in my father's hand had re-painted our home yellow. Actually, my father never came home empty-handed. He always had something, whether it was chocolate, cookies or candy. The number was always the same, four. One for my mother, one for my brother Ahmed, one for me, and one for himself. However, that day was very different. A fruit we saw on soap operas about unsophisticated, rich families had entered our home for the first time. My happiness increased ten-fold. I ran and jumped into my father's lap. He must've thought I hugged him so heartily because I missed him. When in fact, my eyes were on the bag in his hand.

Realizing the truth, my father said, *"After dinner, sweetheart, we'll eat them after dinner."* I put on my spoiled act, *"Now, please, daddy now..."* I persisted, thinking it would be beneficial to act spoiled — it had made my father cave before. But he wasn't having it. I knew I was getting nowhere, so I started to cry. But my father was more insistent than ever before. The bananas would be eaten after supper. My dear father, he never said it, but perhaps he was also going to have a banana for the first time in his life. I gave up and sighed and began waiting. I even helped Mom prepare the floor table. I spread the tablecloth and carried in the copper tray. They chuckled, thinking that my helping was so cute. But my worry was to get to the banana as soon as possible.

On the copper tray were four bowls of lentil soup, and rice in the middle topped off with pieces of chicken. Our floor table was ready. Mom placed the bananas on a plastic plate decorated with colorful flowers. How strange, Mom was acting as though it were an esteemed ceremony that required slow movements. When in fact, instead of this show of respect, I thought the bananas should have been eaten immediately. I ate my soup so fast that I singed my mouth. Did I care? Of course not. But it wasn't time for the banana yet. Mom started stuffing rice into my mouth as dad shoved slices of bread in my hand. I ate everything I would've normally refused to. Even my brother was surprised. He said, *"This girl's appetite is ravenous. Give Hifza another plate of rice, Mom!"* and I shouted, *"That's enough."* The table shook with laughter. By now, everyone understood that I was wolfing down my food in order to have a banana. I started to get angry while they laughed at my situation.

Finally, dinner was over. Dad grasped the bananas and broke them from the bunch one by one. Dad's hands had the grace of a ballerina. It was as if he was putting on a dance performance in slow motion. He handed Mom the largest banana with the same elegance. He gave mom the best of everything. That's why I was sometimes jealous of mom, and how! I would even pray that she wasn't home when he brought back one of his goodies, though usually that didn't make a difference. Anyway, then my brother took his banana. When it was my time, my heart was practically jumping out of my chest! Who knows what expensive toys made other kids feel what I felt for a piece of fruit. Maybe even expensive toys didn't make them feel anything. In any case, the most important thing for me at that moment was the banana in my hand.

Now that it was finally in my hand, I wanted to delay eating it as long as possible. I studied its shape, which resembled the crescent moon that Mom often pointed out in the sky. But my endurance quickly reached its end. If we had another banana, I would want to become friends and play games with it, but there wasn't. Great, but how was I going to eat it? My mom took the banana from my hand, peeled it with her sweet hands and handed it to me with a smile.

I bit into the banana slowly. It was soft, and sweet, and squishy — like my pillow, except you could eat it. If only there was another one, I thought as I finished stuffing it into my mouth, still burned from the soup. I looked at the peels, and, without thinking, reached for one, intending to scrape the inside with my teeth. Dad tried to prevent me, but Mom told Dad to leave me alone. I scraped each of the four peels slowly. This time there was a slightly bitter taste in my mouth. So what, I was still happy. Would I ever have the chance to eat another banana in my life? That's why I decided to hold on to that banana inside me for as long as I could.

All the way until I had a bellyache that brought tears to my eyes. That's right, I didn't go to the restroom from dinnertime until noon the next day. I really didn't want to let go of that banana. Nevertheless, it was clearly evident it wanted to leave me. It was causing a cramp in my belly. I squirmed around and tried to be patient, but it started to hurt much more. I cried, but to no avail. It waited years to come into our home, and now it was impatient to leave me. I got very angry at the banana. I began sobbing, from my bellyache as well as my seething anger.

I started yelling, *"Why do you want to go, can't you stay a little longer inside me?"* Mom heard but didn't understand. She asked me, *"What's going on honey, what's the matter?"* I replied, *"Mom, the banana wants to come out of my belly, please tell it to stay there a little longer. I can go to the restroom tomorrow."* Mom laughed, but then her eyes bulged as she grasped the full story. She planted a kiss on my cheek and said in a trilly voice, *"Don't worry, Dad will bring them home again."* My mom was more precious than a banana. I decided I should give up the banana rather than make her sad. I ran to the restroom, and said goodbye to the banana, though now it looked nothing like what I imagined. Sadly, however, my mother was wrong, and it would be four very long years before we could afford bananas again.

Well, I was the same easily obsessed girl years later. At the risk of becoming ill, I didn't want to move away from the cold blast of the air conditioner, which felt like a fan moving over me, top to bottom. It was the first time in a very long time that I forgot my pain from having to stand on my feet most of the time. I'm not ready to talk about why that was, but this was the first time that, for a minute, my soul stopped hurting. It was as if I was living in dreamland, where there was neither ISIS, nor rape houses, nor death, nor fleeing from death... I had forgotten all of it. I had even forgotten my mother, who had spent seven miserable days walking from Syria after leaving her home and family just so I didn't have to be in that country any more.

I turned my head and searched the room for Mom, whom I had abandoned in a trance after spotting the air conditioner. Her face and eyes were beet-red. Her right hand was on her hip, her left hand in the air. She looked like she was having a beef with the official facing her. Suddenly, she had a bout of the hiccups. And then, suddenly, she began crying. I wonder what got Mom so pissed off in the Viransehir Civil Registry? I forgot the air-conditioning unit, the cool air and the daydream, and ran over to mom's side.

_What happened Mom? Why are you crying?
_I was married, sweetheart, I had a husband. He died, and I became a widow.
_Yes, mom, you know dad died last year. Has your blood pressure dropped? Of course, it's dropping, you've been on

the road for a week now. You haven't rested, and you haven't had any decent sleep either. C'mon, have a seat, I'll bring you some water.

_No, sweetheart, my blood pressure hasn't dropped. This clerk is not talking about your father.

_What do you mean? What's that supposed to mean?

_Well, I had another husband here. He died.

_What are you telling me, mom? Now my blood pressure's going to drop, I'm going to pass out over there. Who was this husband of yours? How did you get married?

_Sweetheart, how do I know? I swear I've got no idea what this clerk is trying to tell me. What the hell is going on!

We two women experienced immense difficulties in order to cross the border and get here. We slept in the mountains and got caught up in dust storms for exactly seven days just for a bit of peace. We fled the clutches of death but were nearly killed in the process.

Our only goal was to get mother's Republic of Turkey identity card that was left behind in her father's home years ago and find a little bit of peace and calm. Couldn't we do without the tears while we were here? My Allah, hadn't we had enough trouble already? Weren't you going to lift a finger for the good whom were reduced to tears by the chortling of the evil? What were you waiting for? For all of us to die crying. I had no such intention! I'm going to die without crying. Those I leave behind are going to cry only for my absence, not because I died suffering.

I was trying to rein in the tempest of rebellion that welled up inside of me. My mother was in bad shape. Her cheeks were all wet from crying. She was speaking in Arabic with me and in Turkish with the clerk in order to explain her problem. I looked at the clerk while mom turned to me and was talking. He cared neither for mom's tears nor my exasperation. He wasn't even looking at us. His nose was stuck to his cellphone screen and texting messages. A disgusting smirk appeared on his face while he replied to his incoming messages. The frequent chirping sound of his incoming messages was starting to get on my nerves. I just wanted to grab him by the dirty, shapeless tie he was obliged to wear around his neck and shout, *"Hey, why can't we get any straight answers around her? Why are you making my mother cry? We escaped from death, don't you get it, from death!"* But I was a foreigner here. My mother was a citizen of this country, not me. I couldn't figure out what would happen to me. As it was, I couldn't articulate well enough in Turkish with all that anger. I went silent, and they continued to argue.

_I'm begging you; can't you just give me my ID card so I can go?

_Look, lady, how can I give you an ID card? If your card is lost, you need to bring me a lost ID card request form from your neighborhood mukhtar office where you reside.

_Look, I'm telling you, I went to Syria as a bride when I was fifteen years old. I haven't been back to Turkey ever since. My ID card was with my father. I have no idea what happened later on. I don't even know if my mother or father are still alive. I had a brother, but I've got no idea where he is. Where should I bring a document for you?

_The records don't show it like that... Look at the records here, look at the screen... Zehra Yaymaz. Birthdate 01.01.1955. Birthplace Viransehir. Date of Marriage: 07.08.1973. Are you this person?

_My name, my birthdate, my birthplace are correct, but I didn't marry in 1973. I was fifteen years old when I got married. It was the summer of 1970 when I went to Syria as a bride.

_Lady, how could you get married when you were fifteen? You can't marry before you turn eighteen! Look, it says here that you got married when you were eighteen. It also says your husband died two years ago, you're a widow and that you have four children.

_Excuse me, I don't have a husband or children in Turkey. Don't you get it? I went to Syria as a bride. My husband perished beneath the bombs. My son's been lost ever since that damned day. My daughter and I are the only ones left.

_Dear Allah, grant me the patience. Lady, go ahead and read it. I'm just telling you whatever is in the records. Look, you even have a widow's pension coming to you. How could you take that pension if you weren't married? How are you going to withdraw this money without an ID?

_I swear, there must be a big mistake. How could I be married here? How could I be a widow? I went to Syria as a bride. I don't have any pension from anywhere.

_Lady, I'm not lying to you. Look, I'm just showing you. Look at the screen. Your husband's name is Abdulkadir Yaymaz. You were married in 1975 and he died in 2012.

_Who did you say, who?

_Abdulkadir Yaymaz. Don't you recognize your dead husband, lady? For Allah's sake, are you putting me on! Do you have a mental problem! What do you want to do?

_Abdulkadir...

Despite all the pain she'd suffered over the past two years, I saw the moment she finally petered out. My mother crumpled to the floor while quietly repeating the name the clerk had shown her. I tried to hold her so she wouldn't hurt herself falling to the floor, but my own pain didn't allow me to come to her aid. I reached out but couldn't grab her. The woman who'd risked death for me time and time again hit the floor with the sound and hardness of a sycamore that was cut from its roots. So, this is what it means when someone loses their strength to fight! Just as all the suffering left behind in order to survive is prowling for an opportunity, it suddenly gathers force and pounces on you. It knocks you out, saying, *"You can ignore us, but you can never get rid of us."*

The clerk ran around to the front of his booth with lemon cologne in one hand and a glass of water in the other. He poured the water and then started patting her face. I couldn't tell whether he was shocked or scared. He wasn't even aware that he pushed my hand very hard which caressed my mother's chin. *"Lady, get a grip, I'm begging you, why did you have to faint on us like that?"* He turned to me. *"Why did she do that? Is your mother ill?"*

Once again, I was overwhelmed with the same feeling of yanking this clerk's tie and bashing him around. He's got the nerve to ask, *"What happened!"* What could I have told him? Maybe I should have explained how my father was trapped beneath bombs in his bread shop? How mother collected my father's shredded body with her own hands. How we never saw my brother who went to the bread shop together with my father. How we didn't have a grave to say a prayer for him even had he died? The things that happened to me, how we abandoned our home, how we got caught up in the sandstorm, how we walked for hours in the heavy rain, the hunger in our bellies, how we waited without moving a finger at the foot of a rocky outcrop from sunrise to sunset in order not to be caught by member of ISIS! Which one was going to whet his curiosity? What difference was his question from asking a lamb that had tumbled down a cliff, *"Which rock split your head open?"*

Anyways, I wouldn't be able to form a long sentence with my patchy Turkish and could only say, *"She's weary."* Mother was really weary. Both spiritually and physically weary. The life we led was not like in dreams at all, and there were tears every moment. We were like rag dolls in the hands of a ruthless child who crushed its head and limbs and ripped open its seams. We were resisting to keep from disintegrating. The only things we could own in this world were our heart, which were constantly breaking due to all the suffering, poverty and hardship.

Nearly the entire building had piled around us. Those who had seized front row seats were talking amongst themselves, making recommendations such as *"Slap her,"* *"Rub her wrists,"* There was also one who said, *"Make her sniff an onion,"* while another one repeated, *"Pour water on her face."* In fact, I even saw a woman crying amongst the crowd when I turned my back for a moment. She was an elderly lady wearing a lilac headscarf and a sash around her waist. I couldn't figure out why she was crying. Perhaps she pitied the state we were in, maybe our drama coincided with her own suffering, I just didn't get it. That's because my attention was struck by the tattoo on her forehead rather than her tears.

My mother also had a tattoo on her forehead. Her own mother made it. I can't say, *"My grandmother made it."* That's because a woman that didn't voice any objections about sending her daughter to another country and didn't bother to ever ask about her again could never be anything of mine. The words said to my mother while making the tattoo would soften me up a bit versus her, but then again I could never call that woman who was my grandmother *grandma.* She should have searched for her daughter on her own if necessary. She should have been as courageous as her daughter, as brave as my mother. Her courage was as much as making a tattoo on my mother's forehead. Because the men of the village had tattoos etched onto the chins, foreheads or arms of small girls who had their first period. My mother was just ten years old at the time. A relative of hers had given birth to a girl. As soon as the sun went down that day, the woman whom I will never call *grandma* took my mother in tow and went to the home of the woman who gave birth. That's because the milk of a woman who has given birth to a daughter was needed to make the tattoo. She also needed soot...

The woman whom I will never call *grandma* brought along the soot of kindling she burned as soon as she learned of the birth. The soot was mixed with the breast milk of the woman who had given birth. When the ink was ready, she took out a needle she kept pinned up in her dress. She began scarring my mother's forehead in the exact center with the needle. Then she poured the ink into the wound with the same needle. The process took hours and my mother was writhing in agony, crying until she ran out of tears. In fact, the woman who had just given birth said to the woman whom I'll never call *grandma, "Why are you making your daughter suffer so much agony at such a young age? You should do this when she's a bit more grown up."*

My mother raised her hopes thinking perhaps she'd be freed from this agony; but the woman who had just given birth was met with stolid silence. After making her final needle strike, the woman whom I will never call *grandma* looked in my mother's eyes, swollen from all of her crying. She then told her ten-year-old daughter the reason for making a star in her forehead in a room that was barely illuminated by a gas lamp latched onto the wall.

"Don't cry, my little meadow blossom. I was no more than thirteen years old when they snatched me away from my mother. While she etched this star into my forehead, my father and elder brother were in the next room discussing the size of the field they were going to buy with the dowry money they planned to get. They paid my father twenty gold pieces for me. I hadn't seen my mother's face even once since that day. I'd touch the star on my forehead with my hand in the morning and look up to the stars in the heavens to rid the yearning I had for my mother at night. I only received word of my mother's death two winters later. I don't know when it will happen, but they're going to separate us as well. They're going to remove my liver and take it somewhere else. You're also going to forget the way home, the water, flowers and air of your homeland. You might get angry with me. But I know that just as I haven't forgotten my mother, you won't forget me. Would one ever forget their mother? No use fighting it, it's our fate. So that's why I etched this star into your forehead. When the pain of separation has descended into your heart, your star will cool your insides, and rid your yearning. Our star will scatter bright yellow light over us. Our heavens will be more yellow and brighter than the gold that separates us. Don't forget my girl, we'll always be beneath the heavens, When we're alive and when we're dead."

My mother would tell me this memory of hers without changing a single word each time. She'd take her hand to her forehead every time it remained empty and fulfill her longing for her mother. Perhaps this poor woman had such a memory as well and started crying as she reminiced. Yet, I couldn't exactly figure out what her tattoo was, which was deformed between her old age wrinkles. I was distracted by a great struggle that ensued to see what was going on in the back by those who weren't able to grab a place in the front rows. Every moment was like watching an action-filled film. They were also right to an extent, as we were no different than the heroines of drama soapboxes with the state we were in. To my surprise, the strange events portrayed in the Turkish soapbox operas that mother and I sat up watching almost every night in our peaceful days were inspired from real-life situations. Was such baloney actually possible? How could my mother be married in this country? After crossing into Syria, my mother never returned to Turkey even once throughout her life. They took the dowry money and sent my mother to our village. Neither her mother nor her father called her since. That's why I don't know my grandparents. Nor do I know my uncles. I don't even know how many I have.

My mom returns to Turkey years later and look at the situation we've encountered. They say my mom is married in Turkey, has four children, her husband has died, and she's got a widow's pension... Oh for the love of Allah! Mom was right to pass out like that. I'm grateful she didn't have a heart attack and croak on the spot. She could've committed suicide as well. But my mother never. Was crushed by the troubles she's faced in her life. She didn't even faint until now. She emerged from every battle fought against suffering and evil even stronger than before. The women of these lands are like that. They have to be so strong as this is the only way they can survive. All problem women encounter in life is no different from a tough workout on the football pitch. This is the condition of endurance in putting up a fight against even greater pains. What agony can a woman who has managed not to die while extricating her husband's severed arm from beneath the rubble be brought to heel? What could possibly be worse in this life for a woman who searched for the body of her son beneath the rubble after gathering the shattered pieces of her husband's body!

Well, the women from our region are like my mother. Children from our region are also like me… We're forced to mature at an early age. We're obliged to behave responsibly and demonstrate steely nerve unexpected from a child even in battle conditions. It's as if I'm a bit stronger when I think back on all the experiences I lived in such a short time. I was with my mother while she pulled my father's shattered body from the debris of the bakery. I was also with my mother when we did search all the streets for my brother. I was all alone the day I swore to myself in the rape chamber where I was locked away, *"I'm definitely going to live regardless of what happens to me,"* and I managed not to die. That's why I'm not panicking at the moment. I'm quite calm as I load words onto my breath compiled in my mind about women's power to struggle and hurl them into space. I'm anticipating the moment my mother wakes up under the anxious gaze of the crowd standing over us. I don't understand why they're so worried. It's as if it's their mother and not mine who is lying on the floor. I'm sure the only thing they'd say if they heard what I was thinking that moment would be, *"This girl is off her rocker."*

Of course, I'm not off my rocker. I've just learned to be patient. Other than adding more pain to existing pain, what good would it do if I sat around lamenting or if I beat myself black and blue. I needed to continue like this if I wanted to support my mother. I checked my breathing and listened to my heart. My breathing and pulse were normal.

It was obvious that weariness, hunger and the shock of this dead husband had snapped mother's body resistance. I was sure that mother was going to pull herself together. She only needed to rest a bit. That's why I really didn't want her to regain consciousness right away. She was going to rest for a little bit even if it wasn't of her own free will. Despite all my persistence, she refused to settle in a camp and get a little rest. She didn't want to lose time by settling into a camp.

She was fluttering like a bird just so she could obtain her ID card as soon as possible and offer me a new life. In the end, she was too tired to flap her wings and was forced to alight on the ground. In fact, she fell to earth. Her eyelids opened just as I was whispering in her ear, *"Rest as much as you want, mother, no need to hurry coming around."* Her coal black pupils became visible. We were now eye-to-eye as we gazed at each other interminably. We poured out our grief to each other without saying a single word. She related, I listened, I related, she cried. *"Let me get up, sweetheart,"* she said. She was in a hurry again. She didn't want to lose any more time. I took one arm while the clerk took her other arm as mother got to her feet. The crowd standing around suddenly dissipated. Even the old lady who was crying a few minutes ago was no longer near us. For them, the movie was over, and the words **'THE END'** were written on the screen. But for us, it was only a fresh start.

The clerk who even said a prayer for mother to regain consciousness didn't leave us. He motioned to the chair right behind us and wanted mother to sit in it. Mother refused to do so. She just repeated, *"No son, just please give me my ID!"* I looked in the face of the clerk, who had left his *"I don't give a shit"* attitude behind the booth. He had the intention of helping my mother, asking her, "Are you going to be able to keep on your feet?" Mother replied, *"I'll keep on my feet, son,"* as she tried to appear tough.

My mother's attempt at maintaining her poise didn't convince the clerk, who looked at me and said, *"Don't ever leave your mother."* He returned to his place like he came, with the bottle of cologne in one hand and the water in the other. I couldn't look at the computer monitor behind the booth as I was propping up mother, but from the speed of the clicking keyboard, I could tell he was rushing to assist us. He got up suddenly, ran over to the printer in the back, and ran back with a printout in his hand.

_Lady, do you know this Abdulkadir Yaymaz? The one who's your husband, Abdulkadir Yaymaz. I mean, the one that appears in the records.

_I know him, he's my cousin.

_Did you ever see him again after you went to Syria? Did he ever call you?

_He didn't s. My mother never even called me, so why should he?

_Lady, I don't know how to break it to you, but I've got some bad news. Both your mother and father died. Your mother died some twenty years ago, and your father passed away in 2007. My condolences.

_If only I could say "Amen," but I can't. I wonder how they breathed their last breaths after they killed me? Okay what about me brother. I told you I also had a brother. What happened to him?

_Yes, lady. It looks like you have a brother in the registry. Mahmut Yaymaz. I looked at his record as well. It looks like he resides in Istanbul. Is there anyone else you might know around here?

_No, son. I don't have anyone else around here.

_I understand. Look lady, it's clear there's been some games played with your ID. You can't fix the situation from here. I'm going to give you the last known address of this Abdulkadir Yaymaz. Your cousin died two years ago, but the records show that his wife and children live at the same address. That is, according to official records, you and your children are living at this address. As a matter of fact, your brother also lives in the same district. Fatih, Istanbul... Go and find them. I don't know if you should find your brother first, or if you better go to the woman who's living with your ID, it's up to you. Go and find out what happened to your ID. Come back to me with one document and I'll issue you an ID card. In fact, you don't even have to come here. Go to any civil registration office in Istanbul and they'll handle it for you. If they don't, then look me up. I'm gonna do everything I can to help you out. Look, I wrote my name and number on this piece of paper.

_May Allah bless you, son. May Allah grant you a place in heaven. May Allah rid you of your worries.

_Amen, lady, thanks a lot. Look, do you have money to get to Istanbul? How are you going to get to Istanbul?

I was so ashamed of myself for wanting to stretch from the firmament to the heavens and scream out to the entire world, *"Are you aware of the shit you're in while we're dying down here!?"* I wanted to become invisible at that moment. I mean, the guy whom I had just swore to inwardly for his seemingly indifferent and rude attitude ended up being compassionate and kind. To the extent of asking us whether or not we had money to make the trip... My mother's silence was enough of an answer for the clerk. Because other than a few Syrian lira in my mother's pocket, we were broke. Actually, mother also had a small purse with gold necklace stashed away in her bra. My father's father pinned it on her as a present when she became a bride. Mother hid it away for bad days. Could there be worse days than this? Yes, there could be worse. Life has taught me this over the past two years. There could always be worse.

We had no way of converting the gold chain lying inside a piece of fabric in my mother's bra into money. We heard all sorts of stories about getting the gold ripped off by con artists in Turkey. We also had no clue as to how much it could fetch. We couldn't risk anything like that right then and there. The clerk also understood our plight. He stuck his hand in his pocket and took out some bills that were in disarray. He started counting as he straightened them one by one. He stacked one green, one pink and two brown banknotes on top of each other and handed them to my mother. *"Lady, that's all I had in my pocket. Go to the bus terminal and tell the ticket seller that this is all the money you have. They'll definitely help you out."*

I could barely keep myself from crying. He was giving us all the money in his pocket, so we could go to Istanbul. I glanced at the note he wrote on the documents and read his name. Then I looked in his face and said, *"I'm never going to forget you for the rest of my life, Kemal Ergan. I won't forget you whether we arrive in Istanbul or not."* He grinned, saying, *"Kemal Ergin."* His name was Kemal Ergin, not Kemal Ergan. I misread it. My mistake had wiped away some of the tension on his face and made the clerk smile. He then proceeded to tell us how to get to the bus terminal, the bus company, as well as which bus, we needed to board. He wrote all this on another piece of paper and handed it to me. I can't remember how many times I said, *"Thank you."* I'm not even going to mention the prayers mother recited out loud. Just as we were about to exit the building accompanied by those prayers, I turned around and asked, *"Do we have to go to Istanbul by bus? Couldn't we just walk there?"* Besides the heavy burden of hitting the road once again, the idea of travelling by bus scared me. How was I going to board a bus, who was I to sit in the seat? Couldn't we just go on foot, even if it takes another twenty seven days?

The clerk who until then was saddened by our plight, gave a slight chuckle as he replied, *"How are you going to get from here all the way to Istanbul, when you can't even walk from here to the district center."* Even if the smiling face of the clerk blew relief my way, the bus journey idea worried me. However, I thought I'd put up with it for my mother's sake. I couldn't force my pooped-out mother to walk just for my comfort and well-being. I should've preferred to travel by bus even if it was possible to walk to Istanbul. I was going to make the effort to sit in the least painful position on the bus.

We waited about ten minutes at the bus stop right in front of the Civil Registry Office. My dear mother couldn't sit on the stop's steel bench, saying *"I can't sit down."* She had such a fine spirit that she never sat across from me even once ever since I returned home after those dreadful days. She'd say, *"If only I could sit down,"* making this self-sacrifice every time in order for me not to be sad. Now it was my turn. I was going to sit down all the way to Istanbul and cry intentionally from all my suffering. I said adamantly to my mother, *"You'll sit on the bus"* as the municipal bus pulled up to the curb. I wanted her to lower the tone of her self-sacrificing for the time being, as we had both already gone to hell and back. She needed to get some rest already and, if possible, even some sleep as far as Istanbul. I knew fully well that she was going to sleep fitfully as she couldn't get my father or my lost brother out of her mind. If only we had a sleeping pill that I could stir into her water on the bus. She would sleep, maybe unwillingly, but at least her body would get some rest.

The bus pulled alongside. Mother got on first, then me. Someone else got on behind me, but I didn't turn around to look. Mother gave five lira the driver, pointing to me and saying it was for two people. She said, *"Bus terminal, bus terminal."* The driver took the money and poured the change into my mother's palm. He gestured grudgingly for us to move to the back of the bus. We were like soldiers taking orders as we moved to the back even though there were empty seats in the center rows. Mother sat on a bench next to the window. I remained standing. I turned my back. I did a double-take as I saw it was the same woman. The old lady with the tattoo on her chin was right beside us. Was she following us, or was this just a weird coincidence? I looked in my mother's face, she did a double-take as well. Looks like she recognized the old woman who was crying over her. We understood the situation when the old lady started talking.

_Girl, where are you coming from, where are you going?

_We came from Aleppo and we're going to Istanbul.

_You look like you're from around here.

_Yes, I left here forty years ago and went to Aleppo as a bride.

_Why are you going to Istanbul, don't you have anyone around here?

_No, my parents died, and the other relatives migrated to Istanbul. They went after they threw me in the fire.

_What fire?

_Never mind, granny, I got a lot of problems. I saw you inside, go ahead, did you want to say something to me?

- Of course, I've got something to say, girl. You're right, I was inside. I saw the trouble they gave you. Your loneliness hurt me. Loneliness is tough these days. I've seen a lot of wretched folks, and they didn't even appreciate that they crossed the border without dying.

_What do you mean, what happened to them?

_Well, girl, first you say you were spared your death, then you look around to see all those who covet your money, your honor and your child. May Allah forbid such things. I've got a brother in Istanbul; he's going to look after us.

_Do you even have the strength to make it as far as Istanbul, girl? Do you think you'll be dealing with someone like that young clerk every time you run into dire straits? Do you have a guarantee you won't run into evil in exchange for each benevolence? There are jackals on the hunt all around us, girl. Look in the face of that youngster sitting next to you. Look and then answer me.

_For the sake of Allah, what are you trying to say, granny What do you want from us, and why are you following us?

_Don't get furious with me, girl, and listen to me carefully. You have no husband; you have no money. You have a good-looking daughter next to you. The brother you said would look after you sold you for dowry money and he never bothered calling again, and you're telling me he's going to take care of you?! I can't leave you looking like this in public.

_Thanks for your interest, granny, but we're going to Istanbul, we're not staying around here.

_You can go, girl, but don't go like this.

_I beg your pardon.

_You've got no money, girl. And just take a look at your-selves, you're an absolute mess. Fine, you speak Turkish, but it's quite evident you've just come from Syria.

_What can I do, granny, we got all messed up on the way here. Do you think we're in any shape to think about what we're wearing!

_You're not going to think about that, leave it to me.

_Granny, for Allah's sake, don't get me all confused, just let us be.

_I understand where you're coming from, girl. Don't be afraid, I've helped out many like you. Look, listen good to what I have to say. You'll be staying at my home as my guest today. You wash up and get yourselves all cleaned up. Then we'll go get some things for you to wear from the bazaar. You can hit the road tomorrow. You won't have to worry about the ticket money.

The bus started moving down the road. We were lurch-ing left and right as we went. I clutched the seatback bar tightly to keep myself from hitting the floor. Meanwhile, I was also trying to pick up on what the old lady was saying. Then again, I couldn't quite understand everything she said. I couldn't do anything but look into my mother's face in an effort to understand what was going on. It was like the old lady's sentences were imprisoning mother in a tri-angular cell. When in fact, mother was trying to get away from the woman. With each thrust, she was smacking the walls of the cell she fell into. She was angry, sad or shocked on the back of each smack. She cried in the end. Looks like they made mother sad again. I shouldn't have let her take things this far. We came here to live, not to be sad.

I got so pissed off, that I swore at the woman in Ara-bic, even though I knew mother would get angry. I shouted,

"What do you want from us?" Just as I guessed, mother gave me a very chagrined look. She gave me such a look that she didn't need to say anything else. Not only my mother, but everyone sitting in the back of the bus gave me some very stern looks. Of course, I paid those looks no heed. Perhaps there were those amongst them who knew Arabic and understood what I said but I wasn't embarrassed by the obscenities I used. Continuing her consternation, Mother was waiting for my explanation regarding the curse words that spewed from my mouth a moment ago.

She couldn't acknowledge my willful cursing in her emotional depression. But I was right. You might be the most naive person in the world, but sometimes life doesn't leave people with any other choice but to curse! So with this emotion, I made the explanation mother wanted in a manner the entire bus would hear. "That's enough mother, I can't take it anymore. What is this woman saying? What does she want from us?"

Mother looked to see if I was going to cry, and her face softened. She said, *It's okay sweetheart, there's nothing to worry about.* The old lady repeated everything she said one-by-one in Arabic. This time it was the old lady's turn. She looked at us inquisitively. When in fact, the woman's benevolence that made mother emotional and got her to cry. Great, but how were we going to trust this woman? We don't even know her name. Where was she going to take us, what was she going to feed us, who was she going to introduce us to, and most importantly, what was she going to want from us? I was reticent about trusting the woman.

Nonetheless, mother trusted her. She didn't look worried at all. I asked her what made her convinced so quickly and made her act comfortably. It was the *"One doesn't get harmed from those bearing a star on her face."* I don't know if they've got similar stories, but from what I understood, there was a distinct emotional bond amongst women who wore star tattoos on their faces. They established an immediate sense of trust despite meeting each other for the first time. Perhaps they had no other choice. This was true, what were we going to do had we not trusted this woman?! We were going to search for others to trust on the way. People you could trust were the most difficult kind of people to find in this region of the world. This generalization could be ridiculous for those who go to bed at night wondering what they'll wear tomorrow. But for us who hadn't gone to bed even once for nearly two years without fearing for their lives, who hadn't had a bed to sleep in for the past two weeks, this was most definitely the boat we found ourselves in.

Then again, I had serious reservations about spending the night with this old lady. Fine, let's go to her home, let's get cleaned up, let's get a proper meal, let's change into some clean clothes, but let's not stay the night. Let's hit the road before nightfall. Let's go and take care of this ID situation as soon as possible. The old lady was sitting in the seat in front of us, looking out the window while I said all this to mother. At one stage, she turned around and said we were getting off at the next stop.

Perhaps there was a really soft bed in the home of the woman with the star tattoo and we might have slept on a cuddly soft mattress for the first time in days. It would have been wonderful in light of our weary, exhausted state of mind. In fact, had they asked me the meaning of paradise, I would've replied instantly, *"A soft bed."* But then again, I wasn't thrilled about spending the night in the home of this old lady. I really wanted to go right away and take care of this ID matter. After she exhaled wearily, mother said, *"Fine honey, we won't stick around here if you're not comfortable. Let's go straight to Istanbul."* I can't tell you how relieved I was.

The old lady was sitting in the seat in front of us looking outside while I spoke with mother. That moment, I looked in her face once more as I tried to understand what she wanted from us. Was I being too much of a pessimist not to consider the fact she wanted to do us a big favor without expecting anything in return? I couldn't come up with an answer, as I couldn't be sure whether there was compassion or deceitful gloom in her face. I'm someone who's overcome monsters, so what now, I'm going to be defeated by the trickery of an old spinster? While this thought spun around in my mind, in putting aside the bad feeling I had inside, I hoped I was making a mistake to harbor such a thought and ashamed of this pessimism of mine. In any case, I would've planted a kiss on the old lady's star, which would patch things all up and put myself at ease.

Mother called out to the old lady and told her our final decision. It was strange, but the old lady was neither upset nor was she offended. It seems like she understood our mental state quite well. Otherwise, she could've gotten off at the first stop, muttering to us, *"I'm inviting you to my home and you're being ungrateful."* But she didn't do that. She said calmly to my mother, *"Fine, my girl, as you wish. But I'd like to see you off at the bus terminal,"* as she turned around and continued to look out. I definitely would've been ungrateful had I turned away this offer to help out. I went quiet and leaned against the bar that held my head up.

My eyes were on the glass, my mind was on Istanbul. I

was seeing homes, cars, colorful signboards, people who were walking and sitting, but I was thinking about Istanbul. If only we could arrive there in that city as soon as possible and if only we could get our ID cards. If only we could start searching for my brother, we couldn't find in Syria. We may be able to find him in Turkey. That's because we heard that some of the injured people were brought to Turkey for treatment after the explosion. We had gone through such miserable days that nobody had any news about anyone else. Ah my dear brother, I wonder if he was still alive? If he was still living, then where was he and what condition was he in?

The three of us didn't utter a single word until we arrived at the bus terminal. As the bus pulled up to the station stop, the old lady said, *"C'mon girl, we're there,"* as she got to her feet. Mother got up behind her. No sooner did we step into the Viranşehir Bus Terminal, when a young man began yelling, *"Mother Leyla, Mother Leyla."* I wouldn't have been scared if he was just yelling, but the guy totally zoomed in on us. I involuntarily moved over to Mother and held her hand tightly. His hair and tie flying out in all directions, the young man who came up to us grasped the old lady's hand, kissed it and took it to his forehead. He did this three times. I didn't understand what was happening, maybe a saintly woman was guiding us in our new country. What was the justification for this respect?

Meanwhile, we learned the name of the old lady from the shouts of the young man. Her name was Leyla. Fine, never mind myself, but mother never even asked the old lady her name until that moment. It was probably because we thought the star on her chin was more important, and we didn't wonder about her name.

While mother and I were anxiously watching what was going on, the young man invited the old lady, that is, Mother Leyla, into his sales office. Without waiting for her response to his invitation, he asked, *"Mother, is there anyone arriving or departing? The old lady with the star tattoo, whom I referred to from that moment on as mother Leyla said, "I've got arrivals and departing"* as she pointed us out to him. We entered one of the sales offices lined up, side by side. Mother Leyla and my mother took the seats the young man offered. The young man showed me yet another place for me to sit. He didn't insist anymore when I didn't take the seat, perhaps thinking I didn't sit out of shyness. Meanwhile, a man sitting behind the booth leapt to his feet and came over to Mother Leyla. He also kissed Mother Leyla's hand and took it to his forehead in the same manner. If this was a custom in these parts, my mother never mentioned it before. The young man who greeted us asked Mother Leyla, *"Who's arriving and who's departing, Mother Leyla?"*

_My son Ahmet, these poor souls have arrived and now they are departing. You are going to send them.

_As you wish, Mother Leyla. What's their destination?

_You're going to send my girls off to İstanbul. And you aren't taking their money either, young man.

_Don't worry about the money, your guests are our guests.

_There's a bus leaving for Istanbul in an hour and a half. Shall I draw up tickets for that bus?

_Go ahead, son. But first, fill the bellies of these poor souls.

_As you wish, Mother Leyla, we're not about to send our guests hungry to Istanbul. I'll pass the word to the steward on board and have him make sure meals are prepared at the rest stops along the way.

_May Allah bless you, son. I've got one more problem,

son and I want you to solve it as well.

_What is it, Mother Leyla.

_You're going to give four tickets for these poor souls. They'll be sitting by themselves in two seats side-by-side. They're totally exhausted.

_As you wish, Mother Leyla.

_I'll cover two of the tickets and you pick up the other two.

_Not a problem at all, Mother Leyla, don't you worry about a thing.

_No, son, I don't want to be embarrassed the next time I come around here, and besides we can share the good deed.

_That won't happen, Mother Leyla.

_Don't make me repeat myself, son.

_As you wish, Mother Leyla.

I won't forget the moment Mother Leyla looked in my face while requesting the four seats from the young man. This woman was not only aware of our shaken spiritual condition, she was also aware of the suffering that persecuted my body. After sticking the money she removed from her pocket under her belt into his, Mother Leyla looked first at my mother, then at me. She took my mother's hand, saying, *"I'm entrusting you to my kids. Don't worry about anything. Get to Istanbul safe and sound. Come back here if you can't find what you're looking for. Your Mother Leyla is here, don't worry."* That's the moment I was once again ashamed of myself. I had nurtured terrible thoughts about this old lady who struggled to bring goodness upon people she saw for the first time. This was the same feeling that Kemal Ergin at the Civil Registry Office instilled upon me.

I think this is the greatest success of evildoers. Not only do they injure our bodies, they also spread fear in our souls. This is a ruthless fear that pushes its victim towards solitude and makes them view kind-hearted people with suspicion in order not to experience the same slings and arrows again. The fundamental goal of those who kill their fathers and rape their daughters, and those who destroy homes and plunder shops is to spread this fear.

I know better now how this fear causes people to become slaves. They know very well that they won't accomplish this by wiping out millions of people. Consequently, their goals are to rule and to relish their rule. They need people who pay homage to them in order for them to savor their rule. What would a king who controlled as much land as the African continent be without any loyal people! I made up my mind at that moment. As someone who had sworn to survive, I had to defeat this fear at the starting line. The evildoers who killed our fathers will never rule us if we don't let them also kill our souls. Yes, they may kill, they may rape, they may plunder our homes but they can't rule, and can't taste that disgusting pleasure. This is also bound to become a tortuous hell for them.

While Mother Leyla embraced my mother, she made another favor that embarrassed me once again. She stuck 100 liras into my mother's hand. Mother showed me the money while she dined at the terminal restaurant. I thought about what Ahmet, who sat sideways in the chair, had to say about Mother Leyla while eating the kebab in front of me. She was the wife of a rich man from Viransehir. They had no children of their own. After her husband died, she began distributing his fortune to the needy. Once the migration from Syria began, she opened up her home to women and children living on the street. That's the same home I was afraid to go to. It was now 5:00 PM and there was half an hour before the bus was to depart the station, as I gobbled down my last bites. And at the end of this short day, I was upset with myself for not kissing Mother Leyla's star. I don't care where I am, one day I'll come back to Viransehir just for this. All my wounds will be healed that day and I'm going to take a seat and talk with her for hours on end.

From: Yusuf
Subject: **What was that pickle ban shit all about? Could it be real?**
August 29th, 2014

It was an August day that was so hot and muggy, I felt like leaping into a pool of hazardous pickle juice. As usual, Hayri piled all the business onto me and was wasting time on the computer again. He didn't disappoint me the moment he started barking like a mutt. He suddenly snarled, *"What the fuck is this shit?"* I was so startled that I followed up with *"What the fuck is that?"* That's the way I was after watching the video that the sonofabitch Hayri forced me to watch. I began uttering weird reactions in such sudden situations. This time was a bit different though. It was as if Hayri was rabid. He got to his feet, sauntered over to the door, went back to his computer, and looked at the screen. *"No fuckin' way, dude, no way, fuckin' shit is that,"* with spittle spraying from his mouth. He paced back and forth once more, his pupils were dilated. What was he so pissed off about? I couldn't turn around and watch Hayri very long as I was waiting for customers in front of the door. I could only turn my back from time to time and saw Hayri in his madness. I really didn't want to pay him any attention anyway. I had no intention of caring for Hayri's psychological state by ruining my own in the process. I was thinking to stay out of harm's way. I was scared stiff the moment I muttered to myself, *"I can give a rat's ass about him as long as he keeps his shit away from me."*

A horrific sound that drowned out Hayri's swearing came from inside. What I saw when I swung around was our Hayri grabbing a jar of pickles from the shelf, slamming it onto the floor. The floor that was spotless just a few minutes had been transformed into an abstract piece of art. Glass fragments, carrots, cabbage and gherkins were everywhere. I went ballistic when I saw that pickle juice had shot out of the jar and sprayed onto the shelves. Just as psycho-killer Hayri was about to snag a second jar, I leapt from where I stood like a stellar basketball player arching for a rebound. I grabbed his arm. *"That's a shame, man, don't throw it on the floor!"* as I took the three-gallon jar from his hand. Needless to say, I didn't care about the jar. There was no way I'd let green plums mingle with the carrots, cabbage and gherkins on the floor. Who was supposed to clean up all the mess! Me, of course.

I still didn't get the gist of whatever it was that made Hayri go haywire. It had to be something over the top. When in fact, this nutcase wouldn't have smashed his prized goods to smithereens for nothing. Hayri had returned to his desk as I reached behind the counter to take the broom. The shattered jar wasn't enough to calm his nerves. His hands were still shaking. He stroked his beard a few times with his trembling hands and straightened his cloak cap. He clutched his telephone with a sudden movement. I began sweeping up the glass shards without making a sound. I wanted to hear to whom he was talking to and every bit of what he was telling them. It was as if the situation Hayri found himself in secretly made me happy. I didn't know what they were doing, but it seemed as though someone was getting back at this maniac. I didn't need to give myself a hernia to figure out who he had called when he screamed, *"You horse-head fuck!"* Great, but he had never hollered at horse-head Mahmut like that before! I guess they were on bad terms.

_The Caliph issued a fatwa banning pickles. Pickles, dude, damn it, pickles! Don't you get it, you horse-headed sonofabitch? The Caliph declared pickles forbidden by religion!

Slamming the phone down hard, he sat in his armchair and buried his head in the screen. He looked as if he was on the verge of crying. As for me, I was cleaning up the place, stunned by the freakiness of the sentence I had heard. While questions were running through my head such as *"What kind of fatwa was this? Who was the caliph and since when did he give a shit about pickles? Did he also announce how many eggs one needed to break for a spicy Turkish omelet? Was this guy a specialist in home economics?"* I had a tough time keeping myself from laughing out loud. It was clear dumbass Hayri felt it in his pocketbook. Five minutes didn't go by before horse-head Mahmut dove into the shop as if he were was waiting at the top of the avenue. This time, he didn't get a *"peace to you, brother"* in reply to his greeting. He met with Hayri's candid sentences.

_Hey horse-head, care to tell me what the hell this is all about? I mean, what the fuck is this! The Chaliph banned the sales of pickles.

_You gotta be joking, you probably misread it.

_Whadya mean misread it! Read for yourself! Should we be thrilled that Mosul was conquered so the state can play with our daily bread? Is this even possible, dude, is it or what?!

_Wait a sec, don't get your balls in an uproar. Lemme check it out. *"Having declared a caliphate after continuing its occupation of Mosul since 10 June, ISIS added new items to its 'illicit and forbidden' list. Regarding pickles, vinegar and dried nuts as illicit, ISIS has banned these items from being sold in the city's shops."*

Horse-head Mahmut went over to the computer, and was reading the news aloud, word for word. He tossed his hand onto Hayri's shoulder. Hayri was looking as sad as if his mother had just passed away as Mahmut tried to pacify him: *"I'm going to check into this. If the news is true, and if the fatwa is really valid, then you have to obey this command. Opposing a decree of the Caliph was the work of infidels. You know very well what non-believers have coming to them, right?"*

Hearing these words that were more threatening than consoling, Hayri's eyes harbored more fear than fury. Horse-head had clearly threatened pickleman Hayri with death. Could someone threaten death just because they were selling fuckin' pickles? Then again, Hayri wasn't into back-peddling. I no longer had any doubt. He loved money even more than his own life.

_Get the fuck outta here, horse-head. What does selling pickles have to do with Islam? This is my livelihood, horse-head, my livelihood we're talking about here. Do you think the Caliph is going to pay my rent and my bills? Who's going to buy pickles from me now? What kind of being a Muslim is that, dude!

I was the one who best understood why Hayri was so bent out of shape even though this pickle ban was declared in Mosul. Although he might not have the need to just say, *"This brother is one of us,"* he was going to lose customers who came around to buy pickles. He was going to lose money, what more could happen? The same Hayri who was once totally ecstatic while the murderous hordes he supported were beheading infidels, was suddenly inundated in an absolute pickle juice funk with the ban declared by the same guys. Moreover, he began to question the interference of religious rules that existed with a human language. Meanwhile, he had nothing to say about horse-head's lax attitude. I don't know if it was because it was a situation that didn't affect him financially or whether it was from the unquestionable compliance with the Caliph's orders, but whatever the case, he acknowledged the pickle ban. There wasn't a single grain of expression of concern or surprise on his horse-head mug. He was rather cold-blooded. It was his cold-bloodedness that was driving Hayri up the wall. How was it that a person couldn't be surprised about this ban on pickles, they wouldn't have said, *"What's this?"*

- _ey horse-head, who from the dhikr community would come around here anymore? Do you think those reading this news would buy pickles again? Which one of them would open a Quran and look at a hadith — the traditions or sayings of the Prophet Muhammad — to see if there was even such a ban in the religion? The most they might do is thump on a tambourine and headbang to the rhythm! Do you think they'd use their heads to learn the basis of these ridiculous orders? I didn't think so!

I was astounded. Hayri finally saw the light of day the moment he understood he was going to lose money. Moreover, he even remembered the Quran and hadiths. He was really livid and could smash Mahmut's horse head like a jar of pickles any moment now.

_What are you saying, Hayri? Don't you even hear what's coming out of your mouth? Best to keep the dhikr community out of this.

_You think I'm gonna ask you what and what not to say, you horse-headed fucker! Tell me, bitch, where in the religion is this written? In which verse is this found?

_Don't talk so much, you think you know the religion better than the wise Caliph? They're busy conducting a jihad over there while you're fretting over a couple of pickles here. What a friggin' shame. You telling me that's what religious brotherhood's all about?

_It's not brotherhood, dumbass, it's called backstabbing!

Hayri uttered his final sentence to the wind. He opened his arms like the wings of an eagle and leapt on top of horse-head Mahmut. They got into a ruckus. I shouted, *"Hey guys, knock it off, break it up for Allah's sake!"* but they weren't having any of that. Why should I lie, I wasn't worried they were going to mess up each other's eyes or heads. They were going to scatter glass jars all over the place and I was the one who would have to clean it all up. Otherwise, I couldn't give a rat's ass about a fight between two lowlifes!

With broom in hand, I prayed that the pickle jars wouldn't break, when I saw Hayri throw a left hook that would make a professional boxer jealous. Then I heard a horrendous crunch that came from horse-head Mahmut's jaw. His jawbone might not be broken but he's definitely lost a couple of teeth. Horse-head was sprawled out on floor. While he tried to get up, Hayri then swung a kick at horse-head, who already had an equilibrium problem. Blood spewed from horse-head's mouth, with pieces of broken teeth spraying to the ground as he spat out blood from his mouth. Horse-head was terrified.

I was forced to try to pry them apart. As I had no intention of seeing more violence and blood, I made a move that I normally wouldn't attempt to do. I embraced Hayri and dragged him on over to his table. I was yelling from the side, "Mahmut bro, get up and get outta here." Horse-head struggled to his feet from where he laid. *"I'll see you later, you bastard, you're finished!"* he yelled as he staggered out of the shop. I gave Hayri a bear hug with all my might so he wouldn't go after horse-head. That heavy stench burned my esophagus again. He was flopping between my arms like a humungous fish and I was afraid that if I let him go for a second, he'd run off and kill horse-head. I mean, I was no Duracell battery. In the end, though he broke away from my arms, what I was afraid of didn't transpire. He didn't run out after horse-head and, he yanked his cloak off his head and chucked it, along with a myriad of colorful curses behind horse-head. He tossed it with such fury that it flew out the door and landed right next to the garbage container on the avenue. He was still a rebel without much of a cause.

_What kind of Islam is this, motherfucker, this isn't Islam! Nobody can interfere with my pickles! Nobody!
_Okay Hayri bro, calm down. Look, passersby on the avenue are staring at us.
_Shaddup and go and fetch my cloak!
_Alright!

Of course Hayri was an ungrateful person. I'm just glad

he didn't decimate the place. I couldn't give a hoot if he railed off the deep end. I headed towards the door to retrieve his cloak, when my faith in the belief of *"what comes around, goes around"* was boosted. Why's that? The stray mutt Hayri had given a swift kick so it wouldn't drink any water was by the trash container. Its tongue hanging a country yard in the summer swelter, the dog had lifted its rear leg and had launched a stream of pee towards the trashcan. I stopped in my tracks. I mean, we should let a dog who was kicked for drinking water pee to its heart's content, right! I was sure the dog wasn't aware of the situation, but I thanked Allah for revenging on behalf of the dog.

I picked up the cloak from the ground in disgust. One side of it was drenched. I took it back to Hayri, making sure none of the pee got on me. Hayri didn't see the dog's work of art outside as his head was still glued to the screen. Nobody could've expected me to tell Hayri what had happened to his cloak. At least I couldn't put the poor dog's life in danger. I just told Hayri that his cloak got wet when it hit the ground. He picked it up, shook it in the air a few times and then wore it. He didn't care about the wetness. The pungent odor of the pickle juice on the floor reduced the smell of the dog piss. That's why it was difficult to discern that he was wearing a cloak that had been peed on, at least from inside the shop. He was so bent out of whack about the pickle ban that he would've never realized it if a dog came around and pissed on him. *"I'm going. Do what you are supposed to do. Look after the shop!"* and stomped out without looking behind him.

He could go to hell in a hand basket as far as I was concerned. The sonofabitch was talking out his crack, like I'd never looked after the shop! He nearly destroyed the shop but not even a one neighbor got worried and dropped by the shop. He tossed his cloak into the avenue and not a single person went over to pick it up! A fucking mutt pissed on it. Naturally, I didn't just say these things. I just swore up a storm at both Hayri and horse-head.

After gathering and dumping out the glass fragments and pickles, I then mopped the floors down real good. I wanted to go out in front of the door and catch my breath, but I first wanted to overcome my curiosity. What was that pickle ban shit all about? Could it be real? What kind of question was that? Of course it was real, but what was the gist of this nonsense? I went over to the computer and began reading the news from the web page of a pro government newspaper, Milliyet.

Date: 25 August, 2014

Headline: ISIS banned pickles and dried fruits and nuts!

Continuing its occupation of Mosul since 10 June, and having declared a caliphate, The Islamic State and the Levant (ISIS) added new items to its 'illicit and forbidden' list. Considering pickles, vinegar and dried fruits and nuts, ISIS has banned sales of these items in businesses. Armed by the YPG in Rojava, 2,500 Ezidi, have been mobilized to the region to put an end to ISIS' occupation in Sinjar (Shingal).

Applying strict sharia rules in the regions it has occupied, the ISIS is imposing the new rules upon those living in Mosul. According to a press release by Basnews, ISIS has declared the consumption of dried fruits and nuts and pickles as illicit. Conducting an operation in the city's bazaar, ISIS members seized the goods of shops selling dried fruits and nut, pickles and vinegar, then sealed these shops shut.

ISIS clothing restrictions were also put into practice. While males were called upon to wear Afghani-style dress, ISIS pressured those who didn't comply. ISIS has also demanded the people to trade their Iraqi identity cards for those of the Islamic State. ISIS announced its sharia order in the city of Mosul, where it declared a caliphate and which it has occupied since 10 June.

HORRIFIC EXECUTION BY ISIS

I swore at those who prepared the news website when I read the headlines of the video added below the news. In fact, I wanted to slam a fist into the screen. I couldn't make any sense of why this news website broadcast the violent video with the title *HORRIFIC EXECUTION BY ISIS*. As it was, the purpose of that execution recording was to spread fear throughout the world, so it was impossible for those employed on the website not to be unaware of this reality. I cursed all those working at this website and closed the page. I was still swearing at those website workers when I stepped outside to calm down a bit. Just then, the roast chicken seller Selami's helper Ekrem was hurrying by in order to get the order he was carrying to his customer on time. He paused when he saw me and asked, *"What happened kanka, who did you get angry with again?"* I was about to tell him when he cut me off, saying, *"Wait a sec, lemme deliver this order before it gets cold. Give me five minutes **kanka**,"* as he sprinted away. I swore at Ekrem too. Even though we were not really blood brothers, we were close enough to call each other *kanka*, short for 'kankardesi-bloodbrothers'. Even though he saw my miserable state, however, he left without even listening to me. Was our friendship really as short as the word *kanka*? For fuck's sake, what kind of shit is that, running off without getting an answer to his question, just when I needed someone to talk to in a bad way!

As he promised, Ekrem returned five minutes later. I started talking without him having to repeat the question he had just asked me. I told him the reason Hayri and Mahmut fought and the murderous videos. I also said that we're living in a hell created by killers who commit murder on behalf of religion and tyrannical, hypocritical religious fanatics who declare anyone who doesn't live like them as infidels. Though he was working for a trickster of a religious exploiter like me, Ekrem objected to what I said. We proceeded to have an argument.

_You can't call those who want to spread their religion hypocrites, Yusuf. And you especially can't call them tyrants either.

_What else can you call a bastard who doesn't live what he preaches, Ekrem? Besides, do you think that despotism only has to do with slicing off people's heads?

_Why should a guy who only talks about his religion and doesn't take the life of someone else be a despot!

_Then why did you go off the deep end when Selami trashed your phone case and threw it in the garbage just because there was an image of a woman on it? Selami didn't kill you, but he trashed your phone case. You didn't make a sound out of fear, but you swore him a new asshole behind his back for an entire week.

_So what, I was pissed off. He took it like it belonged to him.

_Now you get what being a despot is all about, Ekrem? That bum Selami wanted you to be like him even with his preference for a case. He messed your mind up that day, not the case. Look, here's a really easy question for you. If you were someone who believed in another religion, would you be influenced by Selami and what he forces on you to the point where you'd want to become a Muslim?

_Hey, do me a favor and leave me out of this. So, what you're saying is that people should be telling others about religion, right?

_No, but I am saying they should first have morals.

_What's that got to do with it, Yusuf? Aren't the pious already moral?

_Don't be ridiculous, Ekrem. The people you call pious all believe in an Allah they reject a lot more than those who believe in their own religion. If you ask me, it makes no sense for people to be pious without making it a priority to be moral in today's world. This is not an exemplary person. I don't understand why people who compete against each other to have their religion be regarded as the finest go out of their way to neglect this reality.

_Hey, Yusuf, you're dissing the pious again. A pious person is an exemplary person. Because he's an example, there isn't anything more natural than him propagating his religion to the rest of the world.

_I'm not dissing the pious. I'm talking about the pious who have no morals, don't you get it, Ekrem? Now I want you to answer me this question. Which religious book, which words of which prophet or clergymen are as widespread as the sentences of Dostoyevsky or Balzac in this world? The Quran isn't read in christian countries, nor is the Bible in Muslim countries. Jews read neither of them. Atheists or Buddhists read none of them. But everyone in this world, I mean pole to pole, including those places I just mentioned, read Tolstoy, Zola, Nietsche as well. What I mean to say is, there's no need to smash a phone case or someone's head in order to get one's thoughts across.

It's enough just to live morally and with compassion. You might not be able to make everyone muslim, but at least you may be regarded by those around as a respectful and trustworthy muslim.

_Look, I don't know diddley-squat about Zola. So, what do you say, let's go and smoke hookah pipes tonight?

There I was, like a valedictorian giving an eloquent speech on graduation day, and Ekrem's inviting me for a smoke-out. Oh Allah, talk about a narrow-minded world. Let's face it, rather than thinking, they preferred to obey the nonsense of the powers-to-be. He is such a birdbrain, he thinks that everything he couldn't do because he didn't have enough money is because he's a religious person. That's why his world of entertainment is limited to the hookah ritual. What a friggin' waste of time. Leaning my shoulder against the doorjamb and gazing blankly into the street, I decided to hang out with Ekrem as little as possible. Rather than killing time with someone who was the king of shallow thought, I preferred to snooze in front of the television.

I don't know if it was the day's weariness or the stressful moments I was experiencing, but I began dozing off, not in front of the TV, but on my feet. Closing my eyes for a long time, I'm listening to my mind, and when I opened my eyelids for a short time, I scanned my surroundings quickly then returned to my tranquil darkness. I was startled out of my wits on one of those moments when I opened my eyes in fear that a customer could come by at any moment. There was a woman's face in front of my eyes. It was the same exact tattooed woman who passed me the other day in the middle of the night.

I found the opportunity to see her tattoos from a closer vantage point at the moment. There was a pair of diagonal lines with three dots in the middle on both sides of her eyes. This reminded me of my women relatives with tattooed faces back home. But this woman's tattoos were completely different. First of all, the lines were magnificent, like they were drawn with a ruler and the colors were vivid. The dots shone like stars on her temples. Looking at her physique, it wasn't hard to figure out that she was a foreigner… She began speaking, but I couldn't get what she was saying. I could only make out the word 'address' amongst her sentences. She showed me a piece of paper in her hands and continued speaking. She was asking about an address. I looked at the paper, and it was the address of a café on the avenue above the one we were on. It was nearby, but how was I going to give the woman directions?

I tried explaining to her using hand signals, but that didn't work, as if she was going to understand what I was saying with "right, left, go, turn." The woman understood nothing of my hand motions or what I was telling her. I was about to throw in the towel, but I didn't give up. I was going to help the woman out. I was impressed very much by her cordial smile. Man, if only I could speak a little English. Had I known, I would've described how to get to the address with no worries, then I'd ask, *"Who are you, what are you, and what the heck are you doing here?"* But I was determined to help her. I lifted my pointer finger in the air and said, *"Bir dakika."* Either she understood what my hand movements or else she knew what *"Bir dakika"* -one minute- meant in Turkish. She replied grinningly, *"Ok."* I also knew what 'Ok' meant, that is, I didn't know English but not to the extent of not knowing what *"Ok"* meant. I went inside and turned off the computer without even looking at the monitor for a second… I picked the door keys up off the table. I was next to the woman with tattoos before she could say, *"Jack Flash sat on a candlestick."* I was going to take the woman to that address.

I was definitely sure Hayri wouldn't be coming back to the shop. He was most definitely struggling with a killer migrane after all that fighting and war of nerves. I wasn't going to get in any trouble. But I had no idea how I was going to explain this situation to the woman in order for her to trust me. Allah damn it, my internet quota had finished lickety-split this month. I could've gone online from my phone and translated a few words. Anyways, the place we were going was not far away. I was going to take the lady to her address with my flailing limb movements and idiotic facial mimics. I gave the lady's tattooed face a grinning look. I made a *come-hither* gesture with my hand. I proceeded forward, and when I made the same gesture with my hand again, the lady understood that I was beckoning to her. She said, *"Ok"* and began following me.

She was walking beside me after a few steps. It was weird to trust someone who asked for an address and go with that person. Then again, as far as I was concerned, these foreigners were not too fussy when it came to trusting foreigners. They think everywhere they go is their own country. Consider the case of Pipa Bacca. She travelled thousands of kilometers, wandered around dozens of countries, then came to Turkey, hitchhiked in a district very close to Istanbul, got raped, killed and was buried. Whoa, my hairs stand on end just thinking about that. When was I going to be rid of all this pessimism? I mean, I was walking alongside the lady with the tattooed face. She trusted me and was walking beside me. I was the right guy to take her to her address. There was no need to bruhaha over the details! It's not like the good guys are going to lock themselves in their rooms because there are bad people in this world!

The address we were going to was a café on the avenue behind us. We were going to enter a side street just a little up ahead and come out right in front of the café. Meanwhile, I wanted to make use of the few words I knew in English. What difference did it make if I had no English lessons since junior high school! There was just the wonderful trio left etched upon our minds as we graduated from high school. *"What is your name?" "How are you?"* and *"Where are you from?"* My English only went as far as these questions. I don't know whether I'd be able to fully understand the answers the woman would give. I'd be especially stuck if she asks a question on top of those. Whatever, I still asked the wonderful trio. Her name was Anita Tagaq, she was thirty years old and she was from Canada.

The woman looked to see if I was curious and went on to tell me what she did for a living without me even having to ask. She even told me in a manner I could fully understand. She took out a camera from her bag and said, *"Photograph!"* I now knew what her job was. The woman was a photographer. Of course, my curiosity had not subsided. For instance, what was she doing on the streets in the middle of the night the first time I saw her? In fact, the thing I wondered the most about was still unanswered. What did the lines and dots next to her eyes mean? They didn't look like tattoos that were made for women to look beautiful or attract attention. Women who have tattoos to make them look more beautiful have flowers or butterflies etched onto their bodies. In fact, I'd even seen a tattoo of a dolphin on someone's belly. She was an old girlfriend of mine and, as it was, the only innocence she had was that dolphin. If only I hadn't remembered her. Anyways, it was not hard to forget her. I'd already forgotten my old girlfriend with the dolphin tattoo while telling her by motioning with my hands and arms that we needed to enter the street on the left and exit onto the back avenue.

Once again, Anita smiled in response to my hand and arm motions. We didn't speak until the street ended and we entered the back avenue. More precisely, we couldn't speak. That moment I understood how mutes felt. It must be difficult to want to talk but be unable to talk. I want to punch myself for not taking my English lessons seriously enough! And to think I harbored a major dream to question religious propagation strategies! What, with this English?! Who was I kidding?

We arrived in front of the café while I was arguing with myself. A woman emerged from inside before I had the chance to say, *"This is the address."* She said somethings to Anita and they shook hands, etc... The only phrases I could make out of the dozens of sentences and unlimited grins were *"Welcome"* and *"How are you?"* Damn, if only I could understand them properly. The woman who greeted Anita then turned to thank me. Her name was Sevda and she was a photographer as well. She had met Anita on a photography website and together they decided to work on a joint project. She told me in haste so much about how she met Anita and what they were going to do that this was all I could remember. Meanwhile, she told me that Anita was very impressed with my benevolence, that she liked me very much and that she wanted to see me later on. I told her immediately that I really appreciated this.

Anita took out a piece of paper from her bag, wrote something on it and handed it to me. On the paper was all her contact information, including her Instagram and Facebook accounts. As if Sevda wasn't next to us, I gestured for Anita to give me a piece of paper and a pen. In the same manner, I wrote my telephone number, my e-mail address and social media accounts into the notebook she handed me. I had the intention of bidding them farewell and returning to the shop. Even if Hayri wasn't coming back, his meddlesome neighbors might just rat on me to him at the first opportunity.

When Sevda said, *"Hey, why don't you stick around, we can drink something together, then you can go, Anita also wants you to stay,"* I looked at Anita, who grinned at me again. I looked at my watch, and it was still early. I suppose I could hang out a little while longer. I needed to enjoy life while meeting someone who flashed me such a cordial smile. That's because someone who smiled cordially was a type rarely seen these days. And boy did I need someone like that to get into my life in a bad way! Don't let me be misunderstood, but I wasn't in love with Anita. I only loved her as a person. She smiled at me without reservation and I loved her in the same way. That's because there's reservation even in love. You'll expect something in return for your feelings, and your gifts as well... You'll want to be loved and of course, and want to make love as well... But this was a love that was above love. Well, you love, and just love without expecting anything in return. The only thing you get in return for this love is the tranquility that overwhelms your insides. That's all.

When we sat at the table, I told Sevda that I could only stay about fifteen minutes, then I had to get back to the shop. I also added that I wanted to ask Anita a few questions. Actually I intended to ask whatever I could while there was a translator at the ready. Hayri's psycho-killer tendencies passed in front of my eyes, so I backed away from that idea. In fact, not a few questions, but I decided to ask just a few instead. The first had to do with her country. She didn't resemble any of the Canadians we knew. She wasn't blonde and she had slanted eyes. Where was she originally from? I was also going to query her about the two tattoos on either side of her face. Those lines and dots most certainly held some meaning, some purpose. Our drinks arrived while Sevda and Anita were speaking in English and I couldn't even hear a single syllable that reached my ears.

For some reason, I backed out of asking my first question. It wasn't my right to question was being said. If she said she was Canadian, it means she was Canadian. I don't know when it was that I became so sensitive, but I know that working at Hayri's shop definitely had a great influence on my current state of mind. I saw how hearts were broken, how spirits were dampened over rather simple matters in the pickle shop. No doubt there was a bad side to my experiences with working in the pickle shop. The more sensitive I became so as not to hurt people's feelings, my heart was rendered fragile in a heartbeat. This was not a miserable or romantic complaint. I would wish 'good morning' to the driver as I got on the rapid transit city bus on my way to work every morning and proceed towards the rear.

It wasn't long before I realized the drivers were getting snippety and weren't responding to my morning greetings. I was upset and downhearted after not getting any replies. What do you think happened later? I felt I was being dissed. So, nowadays I don't bid them a good morning but just give my pass a swipe over the scanner and then search for an empty seat on the bus. So, let's just see where this sensibility of mine will lead to. I hope I don't go nuts in the process.

It was Sevda's voice that brought me back to the conversation at the table. It was as though I was ready the moment she said, *"Okay, you can go ahead and ask what you want to ask now…"* as I pressed my finger onto Anita's temple. I was expected her to reply with a couple of sentences. I had no idea we were about to engage in a two-hour long discussion that amounted to four lines and six dots. Okay, we can subtract the time we allocated for translation from these two hours, but then again, we still spent a really long time talking about Anita's tattoos. The most important thing was that I found the answer to the question I backed out of asking while listening to the story of the tattoos. When in fact, my questions and answers were interconnected.

_Do you like my tattoos?
_Yes I do, they're quite plain and incredibly straight.
_Just like a peaceful life, right?
_Is that their meaning?
_No, it isn't.
_I'm a native of Canada. I'm an Inuit woman. Have you ever heard of the Inuits?
_No, I've never heard of them. The only Canadian woman I can think of off the top of my head is Celine Dion. As it is, all I know about Canada is from my geography lessons. It's right above the US, it's cold and peaceful. I guess we can call it a cold paradise.
_Well, we live in the coldest region of that cold paradise. Our people and our culture are very different from the Ca-

nadians and the Canada you've seen in films. These tattoos you like are also a part of that culture. Our women have had these tattoos made for centuries.

_Well, I'm from Urfa. Our women there have tattoos done on their faces as well. I mean, it used to be a common tradition, but now young girls and women don't want to be seen on the streets with tattoos on their faces. Think about it, everyone giving you strange looks while you walk down that street. That's why these tattoos don't last long and are soon forgotten.

_Well, that's also why I'm here. The adventure in your country is almost the same as the saga in my country. The young girls and women tend to avoid these tattoos in my country as well. They turn their backs on the heritage of their grandmothers in order to live comfortably in a culture they don't belong to. I'm really disappointed that, like you said, these tattoos might become one of the qualities that will become a thing of the past.

She's not talking just to make herself heard, but we really share a twist of fate with another country on the other side of the world. Women's tattoos in Canada's coldest region as well as Turkey's warmest region are on the verge of extinction. Anita also fretted over this and travelled all the way out here. I didn't want to say this to hurt Anita's feelings, but I thought to myself if only we had such problems to deal with. Excuse me, but the social environment in this country is not of the mindset to deal with such a problem! I mean if I tweet about this on Twitter, saying *"Guys, I'm troubled by this,"* I can guarantee that ninety per cent of my followers will tweet back by saying, *"Screw your troubles!"*

I could sit here for at least another two hours if I continue listening to Anita. But I didn't want to piss off my favorite *dangalak* Hayri by putting my weekly salary at risk. I had to get back to the shop. Then again, I couldn't leave the table without learning the meaning of the tattoos on Anita's face. I glanced at Sevda and said, *"Let her explain about those tattoos and then I have to run."* With her everlasting smile, Anita told me about the tattoos on her face. She only looked at me while she spoke, as if Sevda wasn't between us. That moment, I felt as though I was an incredibly important person. Anita explained and Sevda translated. I was smiling at Anita while listening to Sevda. To an extent, my grins were of amazement.

Truthfully, I wasn't expecting a meaning like Anita explained. The two lines that merged like arrowheads represented the closeness of two separate worlds to each other. They conveyed that death is not an end and, on the contrary, that it is a transition to a new life. The three dots represented her mother, her father and her sister. She had the same tattoo done of both temples in order not to lose sight of both the reality pertaining to death as well as her family ties. The fact she was so fond of her family that she had this etched on her face brought me even closer to Anita. Moreover, I was also fascinated with her belief in life after death. I decided then and there that I had to have a long conversation with Anita.

I was curious about the Inuits. When she said they lived in the snow-covered regions, I asked her *"Hey, are you an Eskimo?"* She replied with a harsh, *"No,"* which only served to boost my curiosity. Sevda admonished me. It turns out that the Inuits don't like to be referred to as Eskimos. *"Most people find this name derogatory because it was given by non-Inuit people and was said to mean eater of raw meat,"* Sevda said. In fact, Sevda was already aware of this situation, if only she didn't translate my question. Of course, it was my fault. The poor woman let her tea go cold while she translated for us. I mean, I even managed to flub this wonderful conversation. Thank goodness Anita took it lightly and went on talking with her never-ending smile.

I got a promise from both Anita and Sevda that we were going to meet again at this café on Saturday to continue talking about the Inuits. I also gave my word to Anita that I was going to find a woman from our parts who was adorned with traditional tattoos. I didn't know how I was going to do that, but I was committed to do so. If necessary, I'd go all the way to our village in Urfa in order to keep my promise. I was quite curious about this matter. When I learned from Nuha that traditional tattoos in our parts were made with a mixture of soot and mother's milk, I muttered to myself, *"Well, I'll be goshdarned."* I've got so many relatives with tattooed faces and I never even once asked them how those shapes were etched upon their faces. In any case, now I know how the womenfolk of both our community's women as well as the Inuit have their tattoos done. Theirs are at least as far out as ours. The ink is obtained from reindeer muscle which is steeped in either seal tallow or soot. Inuit tattoos are made using needles crafted from bone. I learned a lot of things like this.

I even learned that *Inuit* is plural while *Inuk* is singular. I now referred to Anita, who was telling about Inuit woman, as an *Inuk* woman. It was as if I was a part of a live documentary. I didn't want to return to the life I was living just two hours ago. When I saw that Muhsin rang me seven times while I had my phone on silent mode, forget about returning back to my life of two hours ago, I didn't even want to fast forward two hours. If only I could've turned around and stayed at that table. I'm not exaggerating when I say that my brother Muhsin was entirely another can of worms. My brother Muhsin was a brute who wouldn't greet you if he didn't have any business with you, and he was never fine if he wasn't done a favor. Who knows what he was up to! If only he had left me alone during such a fine moment. I got up from the table rather unwillingly. I first hugged and bid Anita farewell, then I did the same with Sevda.

The fifteen minutes I had originally planned to stick around ended up being an hour and a half. I dropped by the register on the way out and paid for the beverages. Handing the cashier a 50 lira banknote, I told him, *"You can pay for whatever they want from this. I'll stop by tomorrow and we can settle up then,"* then I exited the café. I sprinted back to the shop. I supposed that Muhsin had changed his mind after being unable to reach me, and probably wouldn't call again. But lo and behold! His name was flashing once again on the screen. I had registered all my other brothers as *my Brother X* but I only added this brute as *Muhsin* because I didn't feel like a brother to him that much. Allah knows I didn't dis him even though he's driven me nuts on several occasions, he is still my elder. I just pretended to be offended by him and tried to maintain a distance between myself and him. Actually he wasn't supposed to be calling me today. In fact, I thought that he wouldn't be dropping by for at least a week this time around. I had harshly reprimanded him for the first time. I didn't insult or disrespect him, but rather I confronted him with the truth.

What else could I do? There was no other way around it. I shouldn't have made up an excuse and gotten myself in trouble when he called me at night, saying, *"C'mon let's go out and get me some shoes."* Allah damnit, I kind of felt sorry for the idiot. He was so incompetent that he couldn't even manage to buy shoes by himself. I went home, waited for him to get ready, and I waited for him just as we were going out the door while he spoke with a friend who called him. I didn't make a big deal about it. The first bomb exploded while we were putting on our shoes. I looked to see he was barefoot and that's how he wore his shoes.

_Why aren't you wearing any socks, didn't you say you were going to buy some shoes?

_What do you mean socks, why would I be wearing socks in this weather?

_Bro, it's none of my business how you wear your shoes on the street, but please don't be sticking your bare-ass feet in shoes you're trying on in a shoe store. It's fucked up.

_What do you mean it's fucked up, man! Besides, what if someone tried these shoes before me in their bare feet.

_What if, bro?

- Then I can try them on with my bare feet as well. Whatsupwidat?

_I can't believe you live your life thinking up such preposterous possibilities! If that's the case, how about the bums who pee on the streets. Well, if they're peeing, then you might as well join them by taking a piss on the street as well. Whatsupwidat?

I shut up in order not to blow the argument out of proportion. But before piping down, I pleaded him to ask for a trial pair of socks when we entered the store. I really pleaded with him. *"C'mon, let's just do that, what do you say?"* I thought that perhaps courtesy would pry open the door to a civilized world. What a mistake that was. I understood this when we arrived at the shopping mall. As the mall was within walking distance from our flat, we were at the shop in fifteen minutes. He took out his phone and swiped to the photo of the shoes he liked online. One of the staff in the shop went into action immediately and brought around a shoebox within a couple of minutes.

I waited for my brother to ask for some trial socks. That's because there would be some trial socks in every shoe store for strange folks who don't wear socks. He didn't ask for any socks, scared out of his wits a drop of civilization would contaminate his arteries. He opened the box and put one of the shoes on his right foot. I was furious. What he did was revolting. I got nauseous just thinking of the possibility that someone like brother Muhsin had tried on a pair of shoes in their bare feet before me that I wanted to buy. Think about it, those feet are sweaty, dirty and might have fungus. I mean, abhorringly disgusting! And to imagine that this brother Muhsin considers himself a pious person, saying "rightful dues" all the time. But for whatever reason, he wouldn't include that repulsiveness he demonstrated within the scope of *rightful dues*. Naturally, I could no longer put up with this shit!

_Why are you putting on those shoes with your bare feet?
_I'm going to buy them, don't worry about it?
_Dude, what if they don't fit, or if they're defective?
_Then I won't buy them.
_Do you think someone else is going to buy shoes that you tried on with your stinky ass bare feet? Would you've bought them?
_Of course I would've bought them. Besides, what's the big deal if someone else buys the shoes I tried on? What do you care anyway! You're making a big deal out of nothing.
_No way, what you did was wrong. You'd wear that shoe

even if a rat made a nest in it, but keep in mind that not everyone is like you.

_Don't be ridiculous. That's enough. Quit acting like a little girl!

_I'm not acting like a little girl, but you're more like a dickhead.

_Who you calling a dickhead?

_What do you want me to say? You barely take a shower once a week, you smoke like a chimney, you don't brush your teeth, you wear your clothes five days in a row without changing them, you don't even cut your nails. You have as much black crud under your nails as a repairman's apprentice. And when I tell you all this, you try hiding behind the façade of your ablution repulsiveness by saying, *"I'm clean, I perform my ablutions five times a day before I pray."* Yeah, right, give me a break!

I was livid, having reached the point where I needed to get rid of that crap that had been building up inside of me for years. How could a person living in the middle of a city be so filthy, disrespectful and disgusting! Not to mention the fact he's a university graduate with a diploma in civil engineering… I think Muhsin is the greatest proof that a diploma just does not guarantee a graduate a clean and moral life.. Praise the Lord and pass the gravy that those shoes fit and that his filthy ass didn't contaminate anyone else. We bought the shoes and went back home, without saying a single word to each other on the way. I was thinking I'd be rid of him for at least a week. Luck would have it that whatever I thought, the opposite would happen. Case in point, a day hadn't gone by when he began calling me non-stop. I wonder if there was an emergency at home? If there was, then my mother would've called me. Then again, Muhsin persistent calls made me smell a rat. I opened the phone as I was just a couple of steps away from the shop.

_Hey shithead, why don't you answer my calls?

_What the hell kind of greeting is that, brother Muhsin? Us civilized folks generally say *"Hello"* and ask the party on the other end how they are when they pick up. Civilization is a wonderful thing, brother Muhsin, so do us a favor and join it?

_I'd give you a piece of my mind, but now is not the time. Just get your butt home fast.

_What happened, why should I come?

_Don't ask, make it pronto.

_How can I leave the shop, bro, tell me what happened.

_Don't ask so many questions, close the shop and get home now. Mother is calling, and it's your real mother. Just be quick about it.

_What do you mean, my real mother is calling me? Are you saying we have another mother? Don't be ridiculous?

_Come and see!

From: Hifza
Subject: **Life for us was behind this door**
Sept 3rd, 2014

My mother's hand was trembling. I was sure she didn't want to press the buzzer. Unfortunately, she had no choice. From now on, life for us was behind this door. I was behind my mother like a ducking that has lost its brother. She was going to wade into the lake first, then I was going to dive in after her. We were going to live in our new lake without any fear. I wasn't going to be forced to grow my nails anymore. I was going to get to my feet, not because I was in pain while sitting down, but because I had started a new life. Though I might not have had a father to be there for me, being raised by my mother was to suffice me. We were supposed to forget our losses and be happy with what we had.

That's the way I, Hifza from Hasakah, wanted it to be as my mother pressed down on the buzzer which rang out like chirping birds as it reverberated down the narrow street with her henna-tinged finger.

A young man opened the door. He frowned the moment it opened. He thought we were beggars. When in fact it was him with his dirty beard and yellowing teeth who re-sembled beggars more so than us. Once again, I was in an emotional funk because of this crude man in front of me. We were jerking around from side-to-side between the good, bad and ugly like a lopsided plastic ball, and we were still in the exact center of the same oxymoron. Was the reality of this world the bus steward Murat, who hailed us a taxi which brought us here from the bus terminal so we wouldn't get in any terrible trouble in this metropolis? Or was it this guy who waited for his buzzer to ring in order to barf up his inner hatred over the first stranger who con-fronted him? My answer that I might provide this oxymo-ron was still not clear. I might be able to come up with an answer if I could live a little longer. Nonetheless, there was one reality I was aware of and that was plastic balls were the easiest to pop and that we needed to manage to cling to life's jagged cliffs in order not to blow up and disappear. In short, we needed to overcome this hazard without get-ting injured. Needless to say, we were faced with incessant troubles. It gave the impression it understood our effort to avoid any heartbreaking situation and was polishing its jagged cliffs even more than before.

Though my mother was saying, *"I want to see Zehra. Can you call her here?"* his only worry was to kick us off the porch. In fact, not only off the porch or out of the neigh-borhood, but he looked hellbent on kicking us out of the country. He persisted angrily, *"Go on, get outta here, go back to Syria or wherever you came from, but just get the hell outta here. We've got nothing to give you!"* How were we going to prove to this guy that we weren't beggars! He was fidgeting like some housewife who'd forgotten food on the stove, and he could've slammed the door in our faces at any moment. My mother was about to lose her patience with this dirty young man who spoke from the doorway like a coldblooded snake. She leaned against the door and barked out in rapid succession, *"Zehra, are you in there? Zehra?"* Women peering down onto the street from their balconies and men returning home from work, and kids playing on the street before the evening darkness fell all stopped and started gaping at us. Mr. Dirty Beard obviously still thought we were beggars as he wanted to hand us a 1 TL coin from the doorway, shouting, *"Go on, beat it and don't come back."* I was getting flabbergasted with this dirty bearded character who continued talking to us from behind the door as though we were going to do him in. Now it was my turn to scream and shout. I smacked the hand he extended from the doorway and the coin rolled to the ground.

_We've been saying Zehra! Got it? Zehra! She's at this home, so call the woman here.

_What do you want with my mother? Besides, how do you know my mother's name?

_You finally get it now don't you? My mother's been telling you Zehra for the past two hours.

_What do you want with my mother?

I would've answered Dirty Beard's question if my Turkish had been enough and I still wanted to say a lot of things, but I was having one of those moments when I was held prisoner by the few words I knew. Thank goodness my captivity didn't last long. The door opened wide with the instruction that came from inside, *"Open the door son, who's there?"* A woman with a smiling face and a white head covering that came down to her shoulders appeared in front of us. As much as the man she called *son* was flat out rude, this woman was courteous. She invited us in without even asking who we were. She chastised her son for keeping guests waiting at the door. We said, *"Assalamu alaikum, peace be with you"* as we went inside, but not before leaving our shoes in front of the door.

Mother and I knew that our shoes weren't really shoes. They had gotten so worn out on the way here that they were in no condition to be put in a shoe bin. But the woman who invited us in didn't think like way. She bent down, picked up our shoes and placed then in the shoe bin at the door entrance. I really appreciated this woman at that moment. She wasn't disgusted or too lazy, but rather gave our mud encrusted shoes some worth. I wanted to hug her neck and cry, but I stopped myself from doing so in case she misunderstood. I looked into my mother's eyes. She could hardly keep herself from crying too. When in fact, we came her so she could give us back our stolen identities and account for what had happened. Was it this woman who stole my mother's identity card? There was no way this woman could be someone with evil intent. There's got to be another side to this ID business we don't know about.

Entering the living room, the lady host said *"Welcome,"* then she hugged my mother first, and then me. She treated us cordially, as though we were neighbors who had come around for a social visit. I knew this from my mother's neighborly relations, in that while the greetings in front of the door were brief and cold, those in the livingroom were long drawn out, warm affairs. Even this greeting culture showed that my mother, who had spent the majority of her life in Syria, really belonged to this country. After the beggar treatment we were exposed to at the door, this warm welcoming bolstered my belief once again that everything was going to be alright. I sat down next to my mother with a smile on my face.

I was exactly sitting, but rather laid sidewise on my calf. I had leaned my torso against my mother again. The woman sitting opposite us didn't find my lying position odd. She didn't even ask me why I was sitting this way. Her countenance bore the same warmth. I really liked this woman. Meanwhile, I wanted to look in the eyes of that strange guy who treated us like tramps. I wonder what was going through his mind about what had transpired during the last five minutes. But he was nowhere to be seen. I couldn't figure out when he dropped out of sight. Anyways, compared to what we had experienced; it wasn't important what he thought.

_Please excuse my son, he's a bit of a zealot.
_No worries. He thought we were strangers, perhaps that's why.
_No, you don't look like a stranger. You're from where we come from.
_Where did you get that impression?
_It's etched on your face where you're from. You don't have to say anything. Your star is telling me where you're from.
_You don't say…
_Who are you, who are your relatives? Go ahead and tell me why you were looking for me.
_I'm Zehra! Zehra, the niece of Abdulkadir.

I felt pain on the woman's face when my mother introduced herself. She took a deep breath and straightened her white headscarf and said, *"I knew you were coming."* My mother and I were sure that the woman we were looking for was sitting right across from us. We didn't need to ask her her name because her name was also Zehra. We still didn't know what name she used before she took my mother's identification. This information wasn't very important for us. Now it was time for the two Zehras to confront each other and for the fraudster Zehra to revert back to her former identity. Despite her painful facial expression, the woman who lived for years with my mother's name was quite calm. There was a great play being staged and she played the starring role whether intentionally or not. I didn't want to speculate and outright accuse the woman. It's quite possible she was just a pawn on this chessboard. I couldn't expect evil on this scale from a woman who was unable to play the games she wanted during her childhood. My instinct was fortified when she got to her feet and hugged my mother once more, crying a river in the process. The woman was truly in pain.

_Allah bless you, sister, Allah bless you. I begged my husband to have you found. I also pleaded with your elder brother Bahattin. Nobody did anything but leave me in the middle.

_What's your real name?

_Meryem.

_Okay, Meryem, look, I want you to tell me everything, for Allah's sake. I fled death, and I've gone through stuff worse than death in getting here. Why is my ID with you? Please tell me what happened?

_Didn't your mother or your father tell you anything? Didn't your brother say anything either?

_Neither my mother nor my father said anything, Meryem, they never called me at all. They never asked me once how I was. Especially that brother of mine, he can go to hell for all I care.

_Oh Zehra! Allah knows how many years I've had a fire burning inside me. A day didn't go by during my childhood when I wasn't beaten, and they gave me as a bride to someone I never knew while I was still playing with dolls. And as if that wasn't enough, they even thought it was too much for me to live with my own identity card.

_Well, I lived without an ID, Meryem. They gave you my Turkish ID. I never even had the chance to touch that ID. My father carried my ID in his pocket. He sent me to Syria without an ID. I lived there without my ID until now. At any rate, I figured I had an ID in Turkey. When in fact, they gave it to you. So go ahead, tell me what happened and why they gave me ID to you?

It was as if Zehra, whose real name was Meryem, had been waiting for this moment. She wanted to explain everything that had happened and get the chip off her shoulder that had been burdening her for years. Maybe she was going to get even with her dead husband, or her father. It's quite possible, that like my mother, they married her off to some guy she never knew. They shoved my mother's ID into her hands and told her, *"This is you from now on."* How else could this unknown ID dilemma be explained! As I waited excitedly for her to begin her explanation, she got to her feet. I was afraid she'd back away from telling her story. There was no need for me to come up with bad scenarios. The woman's intentions were so nice that she wanted to nourish our bellies before our curiosity. *"We've got a lot to talk about But first, let's go into the kitchen, where we can get something to eat,"* as she showed us into the kitchen. We were hungry and couldn't refuse this offer. How could we refuse, it had been nearly two days since we ate a meal at the Viransehir bus terminal. We suppressed our hunger with the cupcakes the bus steward Murat gave us. And to thing we were going to say no to a hot, steamy bowl of soup!

Meryem also known as Zehra led us into the kitchen. She lit the gas beneath the pots on the stove. While the food was heating up, she then took a salad, cheese, honey and butter from the refrigerator. We didn't need the food that was simmering on the stove, that which was placed in front of us might as well have been a king's banquet. I was in a really good mood when her words *"There you are, we've got lentil soup and green beans in the pots as well. You'll have to excuse me, I would've made something else if I'd known you were coming,"* reverberated around the kitchen. My dream of hot, steamy soup was soon going to become reality. In fact, we were even going to drink hot tea after eating our meal. Meryem a.k.a. Zehra had long since placed the teapot next to the pots to brew tea. We're strange creatures, aren't we? I mean, it's the way a little bowl of soup or a glass of tea lights up our faces when we've got a ton of problems on our mind.

Once we began getting something in our stomachs, and reaffirmed our happiness, Meryem a.k.a. Zehra began telling her story. Her voice was at least as timid as our pouncing cutlery movements. I got the gist of this woman's role from her first sentence, when she gestured at me and said, *"I was around the same age as this girl when they married me off."* That's a shame, they made this one a child bride, too. What right would someone who didn't have a chance to choose while marrying have to speak on other matters! After this point, I wondered what kind of shit her husband pulled behind this woman's back and what she had to put up with. She started to explain.

"I had just turned fifteen. It was a summer day, like today. I was stringing up aubergines on the roof so they could dry. My mother went onto the roof and then stared in my face for a long time. I asked her, **'What happened, mother?'**, but she didn't reply. There were no tears in her eyes, but she was weeping inside. I knew mother well, that's how she'd cry. She wouldn't shed a tear, but she was furious inside. Life had taught us how to cry without shedding tears. I could no longer endure and hugged her neck. I begged her, **"What happened mother, for Allah's sake tell me."** She leaned her head against my neck and took a deep breath. She was like a new mother smelling her baby. She lifted her head and looked in my face again. She said, **"Your father just told me that they're coming from the next village over to court you."** I started crying like mother, whose breath I felt on my face, had died that instant. I was little, but big enough to know what was going to happen to little ones. If a father said, **"a suitor is coming,"** whoever's coming is not a suitor. He's your taker. It's over and done with. Your father had made the arrangement to give you away to someone you never met long ago. The only thing left is the show... That's why I didn't ask mother from which village the suitors were coming from, or who was going to be my husband. What's the use of asking if I was unable to say, **'I'm not going?'**

As it was, my father didn't even tell mother to whom he was giving me. I was to be the wife of a man whose face I had never seen before. I was going to leave mother, my home and belongings. I was going to live with whatever fortune came my way. My father was in such a hurry to give me away that I was to sleep in my bed as a child for only one more night. I was to become someone's fiancé named Meryem the evening of the following day. If what mother said was true, I was to go to *my new home before a month had passed. I was going to be a married woman. My life was going to change in a single night. That's why mother gave me a year's worth of advice in one hour;* **May Allah bless you with good fortune. Hopefully, you'll have the fortune to be with a nice person. Whether he loves or abuses you, don't put up a fight whatever you do. Don't let him hurt you or break your sparrow heart. Don't cry either in front of your husband or in public. A weak lamb only serves to whet the wolf's appetite.**

That day, I had a better understanding of why mother cried without shedding tears. A day hadn't gone by when she wasn't insulted by my father. She was also beaten on a regular basis. Then again, I never saw her weeping, crumpled up in a corner. I asked myself **'How could she be patient?'** *My poor mother didn't collapse because she didn't want to whet the wolf's appetite. While her outside was standing, Allah knew what her inside was like…*

That day, my father was taking me by the hand and giving me to someone else. I was Mother's first headache, her confidant, her road companion. That's why she was no different from a sparrow whose baby bird was stolen from her next. In fact, she was worse. She couldn't chirp like a sparrow and tell her problems to the mountains and rocks. She got up and walked away to make dinner for my father, who made us live with these problems. The wretched woman didn't even have the right to live a melancholic life. I laid down amongst the aubergines the moment mother went out of sight. I winced and gazed up at the deepblue sky for a long time. I felt my tears trickling towards my ears. I was going to have a stranger sleep next to me and not my sister. How was I going to get used to that? I pleaded to the sun, saying, **'I'm begging you to dry me up right with these aubergines. I want to be wrinkled all** *over my body like these aubergines. That way, my suitors won't like me and go back where they came from.'* The sun only dried the tears that had moistened my face. That day, I was offended by the sun. I'm still offended. I don't get out in the sunlight very easily.

I hugged my sister Fatma tight when I went to bed that night. She had dozed off long before with the weariness of the day, oblivious to what was about to transpire. I heard the door creak. I turned to find mother standing there. She laid down between my sister and I. She did that from time to time. She'd sleep with us and go back to her own bed before father woke up. Mother hugged me and I hugged my sister tightly. I turned around and couldn't hug mother. Even if I knew there was nothing she could do about the situation, I was still upset with her. I wanted her to prevent them from taking me away. If was as if mother felt what was going through my mind. She whispered in my ear. I turned back to mother the moment she said, **'Sweetheart, they would let me even if I said I would give my life for you. Don't resent me. This is the fate of all of us. The name of the man who is your suitor is Abdulkadir. He's a presentable, young man. He used to be a cotton laborer, now he's got some fields that he recently bought.'** *I said nothing, mother was like a slim branch, as I twisted my arms around her.*"

Although what Meryem a.k.a. Zehra was saying further embittered our joint suffering, this part of her story really didn't concern us very much. What we needed to know was what happened after her marriage with Abdulkadir Yaymaz. We wanted to know how mother's ID got transferred over to her. It was apparent that she remarried using mother's ID. But why did she do that, how did she do that, who forced her to do it, and didn't she have her own ID? We needed answers to these questions. However, Meryem a.k.a. Zehra had become totally engrossed in herself that she forgot the food on the stove… I was forced to intercede, saying, *"Oh, Meryem, the food's going to burn."* I didn't address her with the name I got from mother. She appreciated that. It was as though I had found something important she had lost and had given it back to her. *"It has been years since anyone has called me Meryem,"* she said. I muttered to myself, *"Life's a bitch."* They deleted your name and wanted you to live with a name that belonged to someone else. It's like they're killing you without you dying. It's so clear that she lived with this agony…

Meryem slowly got to her feet and turned off the gas to the stove. She then ladled the lentil soup into bowls. The smell of the soup wafted my way even before it was placed in front of me. I said a prayer, *"Dear Allah, don't test anyone with hunger."* This was mother's prayer. I'm sure that mother was reciting the same prayer that moment. While spooning up our soup, I asked Meryem a question that was on my mind. How did it happen that she assumed the identity of my mother? *"I'm going to tell you, girl, I'm going to tell you. Your mother's cousin got me involved with all this."* This woman didn't resemble anyone who would commit evil intentionally. I responded with, *"A scorpion wouldn't do what one relative would do to another."* This was one of the proverbs that mother taught me. I snapped out of it when mother pinched me under the table. I made out the woman's husband as *worse than a scorpion.* As it was, this woman's husband was my mother's cousin. I was really disgraceful. I attempted to apologize, but Meryem shut me up by saying, *"Eat your soup, girl."* Then she returned to her story.

My suitors arrived before dawn broke. They brought an

imam with them. I was waiting in the room like a dressed up sacrificial sheep. My sister Fatma was there next to me. I told her to be quiet as I leaned my ear against the door. I wanted to understand what was going on and what they were talking about. Father and my two elder brothers talked with the suitors for nearly two hours. They drank tea and talked of gold, they smoked cigarettes and talked of money, they drank coffee and talked of fields and didn't talk of anything else. Afterwards, Mother opened the door. I thought she was going to get angry when she saw me at the foot of the door, but she didn't say anything. She closed the door behind her. She hugged me like she did on the roof and **'C'mon sweetheart, the imam is going to conduct the matrimony,'** *she said. I was scared. Collapsing to the floor, I recalled mother's words.* **'A frail lamb whets the wolf's appetite.'** *As long as this is going to happen, then there's no reason for me to raise a stink about it. It would be of no use for me to be a pitiful little bride.*

I stood up once again and said, **'Okay, Mother, let me get ready so they can come in.'** *I straightened my headscarf and dress, then sat in the corner mother showed me. My heart was beating like crazy. The man who was to become my husband was going to enter in just a while. Mother said he was a young man but not all young men are good. Mother took my sister out of the room. I was all alone in the room. I gazed at the sky from the window. I couldn't make out the sky very well from behind the curtain. The stars weren't visible either. The stars that were my confidants on the nights I slept on the roof abandoned me at that moment. I was furious at the stars. I was already offended by the sun. I didn't care if it rose or not...*

Someone knocked on the door. I didn't make a sound, I couldn't... They weren't expecting for my response anyway. They opened the door. The imam entered first. Behind him were two old men. I said, **'Oh my goodness! Was my husband going to be one of these?'** *Anyways, the last one to enter was a young person. He was wearing a suit. He also wore a tie. This was definitely the guy who was going to be my husband. He was young like mother had said, but he looked to be at least ten years old than I. The imam, who was constantly stroking his beard, set up shop on the cushions in the head corner. The two old men were kneeling to his left and right with the man who was going to be my husband directly across from him. The man who was going to be my husband didn't even turn and look my way until that moment. He was a little shy. The imam called me over, saying,* **'Come over here my girl.'** *He pointed to the side of the man who was going to be my husband and gestured for me to take a seat. I got up from here I was and sat down where the imam showed me. In just a while, someone whose name I hadn't heard until last night was going to be my husband in the presence of Allah.*

The imam began reciting prayers. Then he asked the man who was going be my husband, **'Do you take Meryem, the daughter of Muharrem, to be your wife?'** *I felt bad when the man who was to be my husband said,* **'I do'** *Somebody whom I don't know has come to my house was telling someone else he was going to take me. What was I, a three-kg. watermelon? I was my turn, and this time the imam, who stroked his beard once more, asked me,* **'Do you take Abdulkadir, the son of Abdullah as your husband?'** *What was I going to say? Of course, I said I accepted. Abdulkadir took me, and I accepted. Then the imam asked the old men, Abdulkadir's uncles, who were sitting to his right and left, if they were our witnesses. They said,* **'We're witnesses'** *then the imam prayed a little more, then they all got up and left the room.*

I remained suspended on my knees in a corner of the room.

I sat there like that for perhaps half an hour. Up until mother entered the room. They had bid my suitors farewell. Father was going to bed, he was exhausted. Of course, he's exhausted, I'd get exhausted too if I had done all that bargaining. Instead of putting it on my finger, they gave the engagement ring to father, but I was now engaged. Even more, I was engaged by an imam. My suitors were now worried about organizing the wedding before autumn. I was able to stay at home for another three weeks. After the engagement, I could only see Abdulkadir at the wedding. He didn't even once come by and see how I was doing. I thought he didn't drop by because he was dealing with those famous fields of his. That wasn't so, as he was too embarrassed to come. He told me the night of our wedding, saying, **'You gotta admit, we tyrannized you. We didn't ask if you were willing or not.'**

I had finished my soup some time ago, and I was twirling my spoon in my bowl so that Meryem wouldn't give a break. It was as if the bowl wasn't empty... I wanted Meryem to finish telling us what went down without interruption. However, when her last sentence contradicted the Abdulkadir Yaymaz in my head, I was forced to interrupt. For what I understood, he was the one who seized mother's ID and forced this woman to live with someone else's ID for the rest of her life. How was it that a man who stole a woman's ID and the childhood of another woman could be so sensitive to say, *"You gotta admit."* I couldn't keep to myself what was going through me mind. I asked Meryem frankly.

She merely repeated that she would explain everything if I remain patient. She was so tactful while speaking, I just couldn't say, *"How can I remain patient?"* While swapping our soup bowls for plates full of hot green beans, it was like she was reading the impatience on our faces. After sitting back down, she looked in our eyes for what seemed like an eternity. She was acting as though it was me rather than my mother who was the victim of this game. *"Patience is a virtue, dear, I'm going to tell you the whole story. You know, I have a son around your age. May Allah protect him."*

I went silent when she said, *"He's the only one of my children who doesn't know the truth. If you allow me to call him in here, I want him to hear what I'm going to say. The father explained it before to the older kids and now it's my turn to tell Yusuf. One doesn't know when the Grim Reaper might come around, dear, so the best time is now. So let's have my Yusuf join us then I'll continue telling my story, okay dear?"* I put myself and mother aside and thought of Yusuf. I wonder what he's going to do when he learns his mother is Meryem? Will he be able to find to find Zehra's warmth in Meryem? Though I still don't know the details, what sort of reaction will he have when he learns of his father's deceptive games?

My hip ached from sitting in the hard chair all this time. I was thinking to myself, wouldn't it be wonderful if we could go over to the sofa in the living room. Once again, it was as though Meryem had read my thoughts when she said, *"C'mon let's go into the living room, we can drink our tea there."* Actually, this is normally what hospitality is all about. The meal is eaten, then afterwards, we'd move on over to comfortable armchairs, where the conversation would be accompanied by tea. So, why was I so surprised and appreciative of this? Because we needed it, that's why.

As we moved into the living room, Meryem shouted, *"Muhsin"* a few times. The pain in the ass who tried to kick us off the porch emerged from the back room. He had a hand in his pocket as he leaned against the living room door, asking, *"What do you want, mom?"* I found it rather strange for such a tactful woman to have such a rude son. That's Allah for you… I don't know why, but there's not a thing that is given to anyone fully in this life! Not even Meryem's half-joking, *"Son, I'd like to introduce you to your real mother, go over and kiss her hand and welcome her!"* could alter Muhsin's frozen facial expression. He only said halfheartedly, *"Welcome."* Then he turned to his mother and said, *"What's going to happen now?"* Meryem replied, *"What do I know, just go and call Yusuf. Have him come, and I guess we'll figure out what to do then…"*

From: Yusuf
Subject: **Women and girls are spoils of war**
Sept 05th, 2014

Following the horror, I experienced at the pickle shop in the morning, I had fallen into another nightmare in my own home the same night. After a long argument, the final conversations I had with mother went like this:

_You messed me up mother.
_What do you mean by that, son?
_You lied, mother. You lied to all of us. What's even worse is that you lied to yourself your entire life.

I had no strength to endure this much of a shock in a single day. I preferred to go to my room and sleep as soon as possible in order to rid myself of the nightmare I lived while sober. When I opened my eyes, mother was across from me. She was asleep in the chair next to my bed with her neck drooping to the side. What shame, she was up all night on that uncomfortable chair because of me. Oh mom, I hurt you deeply last night. There was no need for me to sit and ponder about it later, I knew I was breaking her heart as I uttered those words. But then, I was right. After what had happened during that pickle shop hell, the things I heard the moment I arrived at home drove me up the wall. Nobody could expect me to act nonchalantly in such a situation. Mother in particular could not expect such behavior from me. Because it wouldn't have entered my mind that she'd be the only one in this life to accept such a trick.

There must've been a serious reason behind accepting to live with someone else's ID. I might've found the answer I was looking for had I been a little more patient. I didn't give the poor woman a chance. I ranted and raved a bunch of questions, and then shut myself up in my room like a spoiled kid without listening to the answer to any of them. After not saying a single word to *dangalak* Hayri, I took out all my frustrations on mother. So, there was the consequence across from me, a mother who was up all night on a wooden chair in order to tell her son what had happened.

As a kid, I couldn't sleep without holding mother's hand. Her hand was a sort of armored plating for me. The darkness was impenetrable armor that gave me strength and assurance to counter kidnapping monsters and bad dreams… I was telling myself that now was exactly the time to hold that hand again. It was my turn. I couldn't leave mother in these tough times. I had to give her strength so that she could rid herself of this calamity she was forced to conceal for years. I had to give her a taste of the sense of trust now that she didn't deny me even in her sleep when I was a kid. I reached out to mother's hand holding rosary beads, grasping her fingers that hung between the rosary beads like delicate leaves. She woke up and looked into my eyes, saying, *"I didn't do anything to embarrass you, my dear son."*

Tears began to trickle from the eyes that had just opened. I sat up quickly from my place. I hugged her neck and said, *"I know, mom. I'm just pissed to see you in such a screwed up situation. But I know for a fact, that whatever you did, you did it for us. C'mon, let's have a nice breakfast, we'll talk."* Just as she did when I was a kid, she sniffed my neck and planted a sweet kiss on my cheek, saying, *"Okay, my dear."* I looked in her eyes, they were moist, but there was trust in them. My conscious was comforted to an extent.

Breakfast table was more crowded than other days. At the table were mother, my three elder brothers, and the two guests to whom I didn't utter a single word after saying *welcome* last night. I was a bit embarrassed, and I smiled at our guests as soon as I sat at the table in an effort to have my rudeness forgiven, asking them how they were, as if the rudeness I demonstrated last night never occurred. Like she did last night, the guest girl, whose name I refrained from asking, was sitting sidewise on the chair, and would've fallen off if she was given a little shove. While averting my glances so that she wouldn't misunderstand me, the tattoo on her mother's chin caught my eye. For a second, I recalled Anita's smiling face.

The woman I was looking for was sitting right across from me. I was thrilled that I was able to quickly fulfill the promise I made to Anita. I didn't know at that moment if our guest would like to talk with Anita or not. I thought I could convince her somehow, but there was a life or death situation we needed to solve first and this situation needed to be resolved at this breakfast table. I'm sure mother wanted this the most. It was obvious from the way she filled the teacups and sat down hurriedly. She took a sip of her tea and then jumped right into the subject:

I was married off at the beginning of autumn. It was as if I wasn't the bride whom they pulled a red covering over my head with a gaudy dress they made me wear. I was a poor, wretched girl who was being sent from her home accompanied by a drum and shrill horn. I wasn't of the age to have an official marriage ceremony. I was very unhappy when I was leaving home, but thank Allah blessed me with a nice husband. He didn't disappoint me for even one day. But he also never mentioned anything about an official marriage.

*One night, while eating dinner, I couldn't endure it any longer and asked him. I had to ask him, because I had turned eighteen and had born him two children. I asked him, **'Aren't we going to have an official wedding? Okay, forget about me, how are we going to register the kids at the census bureau? How do you expect these children to live without ID cards?'** I was waiting for him to respond immediately, but Abdulkadir was so calm. He dropped his spoon on the table slowly. Then he picked up the water glass in front of him with difficulty, as though it was a cannonball and drank from it. Finally, he put the glass on the table, bent his head to the ground and said, **'I'm married.'***

*I was devastated. I exclaimed, **'Who is your second wife Abdulkadir? Where is she? Where does she live? How could you have done this terrible thing to me?"** as I started crying. **I no longer cared about mother's advice; "Don't cry in front of your husband or anyone else.'** I flung my spoon into the soup in front of me, and just as I was getting up from the table, Abdulkadir grabbed my arm, asking, **'Sit the hell down, where do you think you're going?'** I had nowhere to go. I was just going to go out in front of the door and do my crying. However, Abdulkadir didn't let me, saying, **'What second wife, I have only one wife and that's you. I am only*** *married on paper, if only I'd told you everything before we got married.'* I shut up when your father said, *'You don't need to, you can take care of everything later, I am so sorry.'* I couldn't figure if I should damn my father for the crap, he put me through or my husband for the secret he hid from me. So, I sat and cried while I listened to my husband.

Before we were married, Abdulkadir, like everyone else living in our region, would go to Adana city to pick cotton during the summer. In 1975, the government introduced a land reform program in Sanliurfa while Abdulkadir was out picking cotton in Adana. The state had begun giving land to those who didn't own vineyards, gardens or fields. Abdulkadir's cousin, Bahattin, who's also Zehra's elder brother, sent Abdulkadir a letter, in which he wrote, **'Hurry back home, the state's giving out land.'** Abdulkadir returned to Sanliurfa without getting paid for the cotton he picked. Who wouldn't want to pick cotton in their own fields rather than someone else's fields! He wanted to file an application for a field as soon as he arrived in Sanliurfa. The door was slammed in his face even before he could get inside a state office. He learned that the land reform was only for married couples. Abdulkadir was out both his money in Adana, as well as that from the field. That's just when Bahattin rang Abdulkadir and gave him a bright idea. He said, **'You know, we married Zehra off to Syria. Her ID certificate is in my father's house. Let's get you married with that ID certificate, what do you say! You will be able to get your field that way. Then you can go and get a divorce. You will give me my share as well.'**

Abdulkadir thought he wouldn't be able to get married without Zehra and rejected Bahattin. He decided to go back to Adana with the hope of finding work in another cotton field. Bahattin was one not to miss the chance to get his share of *the field action.* **'Don't worry, the census registry manager is my friend, let me handle your marriage business'** *he said as he got Abdulkadir to change his mind. He kept his word and went to the census office without Zehra, just showing her ID certificate and got them married.*

I couldn't resist, so I cut in, *"How can that be, mom! How do they conduct marriage ceremonies without the owner of the ID being there?"* When in fact, the first rung of the chain that trashed our peace today formed in the vulgarity of this market shopping spree. Back then, as all procedures at the census bureaus were logged in by hand, all sorts of dodgy business could be easily carried out. The census office manager took care of the marriage procedure because Zehra didn't show up in the records as *married*. The census office director, who fell for a bottle of raki, wrote the names of two officials as witnesses who worked for the bureau. He also had his sister sign the document instead of Bahattin. As a result, my father, who couldn't even get a pass to a soccer game at that time, was officially married with just a single process.

After mother told us about father's married life, she got up from the table holding her teaglass. She went out of the kitchen thinking to get another glass of tea. We all looked behind her in tepid silence. Then we all drank our tea in the same sullen atmosphere and nibbled our breakfast. While waiting to see who would break the silence, Mother reappeared holding an empty teaglass, an ID certificate and something like a small notebook. She put the ID certificate in front of Zehra, then went over to the stove without saying a single word and filled her glass with tea. She turned around in slow motion and took her seat. Breaking the silence at the table with, *"Zehra, that's your ID cer-*

tificate. That's my photograph on it, but the card is yours." I looked at Zehra, who had picked up her pink-colored ID certificate and was inspecting it. It was obvious from my swallowing that I was having a tough time keeping myself from crying. Hifza was also looking at the ID certificate with his head leaning against his mother's shoulder. Once more, Hifza's condition caught my attention. She was leaning on her mother throughout breakfast. Now I was certain she had some sort of handicap. I guess it would be shameful if I asked her what her handicap was without being introduced properly. I looked into Hifza's face once more without her noticing and left this matter to another time. However, I couldn't leave the shine in Hifza's face to one side. There were sparks in Hifza's face that shot fire into my heart.

My mother switched my curiosity that slid to Hifza back to our actual subject. She showed me the notebook in her hand, saying, *"Look, this is my ID certificate."* I was seeing this sort of ID certificate for the first time. The old ID certificates were like small notebooks. I picked it up, it resembled a passport. It was written *Nufus Huviyet Cuzdani* on it and the inner pages were handwritten. Zehra said her ID certificate used to be just like that. When my father wouldn't give her an official divorce, my mother began using Zehra's ID certificate, and hid away her old ID certificate.

I took a good long look at mother's old ID certificate. I was really curious. I wonder how many times the IDs were changed and how many censuses were taken over the years. Didn't anyone ask where the owner of this ID certificate was, didn't anyone care why this ID certificate wasn't renewed? Mother's reply didn't surprise me much. Whenever my immoral grandpa had state business, he'd say that mother went to Syria as a bride and that she was never coming back. That's why mother's ID certificate remained as good as new.

I also asked mother why she didn't divorce father. I mean, you'd think that it would be as easy getting a divorce as it would be getting a fake marriage! While I was conducting this interrogation in my inner world, mother picked up the teapot that was waiting on the stove at low flame and was filling the glasses of everyone at the table. She began telling about father's attempt to divorce while filling Zehra's glass with tea.

*As he was afraid that a fake marriage would be noticed, Abdulkadir said he wouldn't lift a finger to get a divorce, until the day I raised a big stink. That's when he asked me for forgiveness once more. It burned him up to see me sad. As it was, the time had come to get the kids registered at the census office. Our oldest son was more than two-year-old, and little Yahya was three months. Neither of them had IDs. Abdulkadir said, **'Let's see what's in the cards, and rid ourselves of this trouble'** and the next morning he headed out to the courthouse instead of the cotton field. He gave the prosecutor the divorce petition he had written by a street petition writer. While recording his statement, the prosecutor asked Abdulkadir whether or not Zehra wanted a divorce. How would have he'd known that was in Syria, married to another man! Abdulkadir knew the moment he told the prosecutor, **'Zehra also wants a divorce'** that he'd never get a divorce. That's because the prosecutor said, **'It doesn't matter whether she wants a divorce or not, she has to be present in court to give her statement, otherwise you'll never get a divorce.'** When he heard this, Abdulkadir said, **'Let me talk this over again with her,'** and tried to take back his petition. The prosecutor admonished him, saying, **'Are*** *you trying to put one over on the state?'* But in the end, he handed Abdulkadir back his petition, saying, *'You better not show up here again.'*

Understanding he wasn't going to get a divorce, Abdulkadir went straight over to Bahattin's place as soon as he left the courthouse. Telling him what had transpired down at the courthouse, he demanded that Bahattin get him out of the hot water he found himself in. Bahattin paid him no attention. Saying, **'Everything was peachy keen when you got your field, but now you have to deal with it yourself. It's none of my business,'** *as he kicked Abdulkadir off his porch. He also wanted the thirty per cent cut back he had paid him from his harvest income, telling him he wasn't going to pay him another cent. Hearing that he wasn't going to get any more money, Bahattin threatened him, telling the prosecutor about his illegal marriage.*

Abdulkadir retorted with, **'Hey, the census manager is your friend, not mine, you're the one who bribed with him a bottle of raki, you're the one who got a cut from the harvest, tell him whatever you want, if I go down, you're going down with me.'** *Bahattin saw that this was an expensive proposition, and invited Abdulkadir, whom he had just kicked off his porch, back into the house. Besides, he had another trick up his sleeve to keep him from losing his share in future harvests as well as to save his own butt from the fake wedding headache. He said to Abdulkadir,* **'It doesn't matter, Zehra's in Syria, she'd only come here if all hell broke loose. She doesn't need her ID certificate in Syria. Your wife can use Zehra's ID from now on, there's nothing to worry about!'**

When he arrived home that night, Abdulkadir's face was beet-red. He went over to the corner cushion and sat down without saying a word. I went into the same room and sat *across from him. Despite the unhappiness on his face, I was looking straight in his eyes, thinking he might have some good news for me. He took out his cigarette case from his pocket and rolled himself a cigarette. He always wanted tea whenever he rolled a cigarette, but he didn't ask for any that day. He didn't even ask for an ashtray to tap his ashes into. With every blow of smoke that filled his lungs, he tapped the ashes of his cigarette into his palm. After exhaling his final breath, he tried putting out his cigarette in his palm. I shouted, **'What are you doing?'** as I leapt from where I sat and grabbed the cigarette from him. I then dumped the ashes that were in his palm into my hand. Not wanting to have Abdulkadir's hand burned, I ended burning my own hand with the cigarette instead. But the cigarette burn didn't hurt me as much as the tears that poured from Abdulkadir's eyes.*

*Abdulkadir cried as he told me what had happened. He said there wasn't anything else to do except to take Bahattin's advice. Then he removed Zehra's ID certificate from his pocket and said, **'This is yours now. You're Zehra now.'** Taking the ID of a woman who married my husband before me was absolutely devastating. It meant I wasn't going to get married officially with my own name and that the name of another woman was going to be written on the ID certificates of my children. But I had no other choice but to accept this. My husband was desparate and so was I. I couldn't leave him as I had no other place to go if I did. Both of us accepted this situation unwillingly. However, we both pondered the entire day how we were going to have my photograph added to Zehra's ID certificate.*

Again, it was Bahattin who came up with the solution. He must've been worried about his share he was supposed to receive from the harvest as he came pounding on our day before the break of day. He charged inside, saying that Zehra's

ID certificate needed to be renewed. When we asked how this was going to happen, he picked up Zehra's ID and opened it to the first page, saying, **'Look, there's no photo. There's just a stamp where the photo's supposed to be. That's because no photo is attached to ID certificates until the age of fifteen. Zehra's photo wasn't added to the ID as she went to Syria as soon as she turned fifteen. What does this mean? It means there's no photo of Zehra at the census bureau. Don't you remember, Abdulkadir, we almost couldn't get you married because there wasn't Zehra's photo.'**

Abdulkadir and I were listening to Sneaky Pete Bahattin like death-row prisoners waiting for a last-minute stay of execution. As there wasn't much of an age difference between Zehra and me, the birthdate on the ID wasn't going to raise eyebrows with the photo. We did whatever Bahattin said. We went to the photographer's the same day. Bahattin disappeared while we were inside having my photo shot, only to show up later on with a black plastic bag in his hand. **'He's up to no good again,'** *I muttered to myself. I asked Abdulkadir what was in the bag. He replied,* **'It's the manager's medicine.'** *I understood what Abdulkadir meant after we called on the census bureau director. Bahattin when into the room of the census director together with Abdulkadir. I waited outside. The census director played hard to get but was swayed by the bottle of raki poking out from Bahattin's black bag. After waiting nearly two hours, they stuck an ID certificate with Zehra's name and a photo that belonged to me in my hands. Well, we complied with Bahattin's plan and it's gotten us into today's mess. Now I have no idea what's going to happen now.*

I would've never believed this story had mother not told it. Then again, there were still a few matters that confused me regarding this ID dilemma, and I wasn't about to let anyone leave the table without getting satisfactory answers to my questions. After mother, it was Zehra's turn to tell her story. She had to explain why she left her ID certificate in Turkey, and why she went after her ID after all these years. I looked into Zehra's face; all her attention was on the ID card in her hand. It was as if she was ridding herself of all the pent-up longing with the ID she was reunited with after all these years. I fired off my first question without any compunction.

_Aunt Zehra, why did you leave your ID at your father's home? Did you think your passport would be enough?

_What do you mean *passport* son, I never had a passport.

_So how did you pass through the border without a passport, aunt Zehra? The one you said wasn't possible.

_Do you think there was a border gate for us back then, son? We were loaded onto the back of a donkey and passed over paths cleared of mines used by smugglers on into Syria.

_Aunt Zehra, pardon me, but I just can't believe what you're telling me. Fine, you were smuggled into Syria, so how did you live in Syria without a passport or an ID for all those years?

_Son, Syria wasn't giving ID to foreign brides like me. None of us women like me who came from abroad had any ID. Our husbands and children had them, but not us. As it was, women like me who never left the home had no need for them anyway. You couldn't go to a state office, nor school … If you were ill, you had to recover at home, if you died, you were buried in a space in the neighborhood cemetery. My ID would've been a gravestone had this war not broken out, and had I not come around here again.

_Instead of waiting for a gravestone, why didn't you want your ID in Turkey, Aunt Zehra? Had you taken your ID with you, none of us would be in this mess we are in today.

_Son, I'm touching my ID certificate for the first time now. My father never showed me my ID card even once. He never called nor asked about me after he sent me off to Syria. How was I supposed to come back around here as a full-grown woman?

_Well, you're here now aren't you? How did that happen?

If only we could delete at the same speed words that make us regretful the moment, they leave our mouths. That's because my last words upset aunt Zehra. Mother cut in, saying, *"Hey, it's not the woman's fault, son, why would you say such a thing?"* My elder brother, Harun, who'd been eating breakfast quietly ever since he arrived, couldn't resist adding his two cents, roaring, *"It's the men's fault if she couldn't come before, and it's the men's fault if she was forced to come here now. Okay, so you're not familiar with the social environment you were brought up in, is it because you didn't understand what my mother said that you disregard women in a culture dominated by men? What are you so surprised about that makes you talk nonsense?"*

Talking as though he was constantly explaining a lesson from his days as a teacher, I couldn't protest my elder brother Harun this time, saying *"Go and tell that to your students,"* because he was right. I had that lesson coming to me. I apologized to aunt Zehra. I didn't mean to hurt her at all. She was such a naive woman that she replied, *"Don't get down on yourself, Yusuf, I know you don't harbor any bad feelings towards me. I also know that you deserve an answer to the question you asked."* Even though I insisted it wasn't necessary, aunt Zehra answered my rude question. *"I was fifteen when I went to Hasakah as a bride and I returned here almost forty years later. You tell me Yusuf wouldn't you think that stone would turn to dust from all that longing all this time!"*

I didn't know how to reply to aunt Zehra's question. I was so embarrassed that not a single word emerged from my mouth. I could only nod my head slightly. I continued listening to aunt Zehra. The more she spoke, the more I dug my own grave. It wasn't possible to feel anything else but embarrassment after hearing these words that poured from aunt Zehra's mouth: *"I was waiting patiently during the early days when I went as a bride for my father to come and take my away or for my husband to take me away. My husband didn't take me away. Forget about taking me away, my father didn't even send his greetings. As it was, I never expected my elder brother to commit such a humane gesture. My mother also knows that we were raised to know that a woman couldn't even go to the village without having a man at her side. How was I going to come to Turkey as a single woman? Who was I to rid my yearning with if I came? With those who tossed me over the border and then forgot about me!"*

Melancholy enveloped me as I figured it'd be better if I didn't gouge aunt Zehra's wound out further. However, I still had some unanswered questions rolling around my head. As it was, I was from Sanliurfa and at least I was following what went on at the border from the news. In fact, while aunt Zehra was talking, I recalled the tradition of border bairam greetings I'd known from my childhood. I refreshed my memory from my cellphone by running a search on Google about our eid al-fitr and eid al-adha traditions. While they spelled out the borders between Turkey and her neighbors, the treaties signed in the 1920's had divided relatives who were living in the border districts. Barbed wire had been installed between our relatives who were just a shout or a wave away from each other. That's why these families had been exchanging eid greetings from behind the borderline barbed wire all this time. They'd toss eid gifts such as tea, sugar and toys to each other over the emplacements. Later on, the barbed wire hassle was lifted.

I remembered the exact year once I noticed the news that appeared on Google. An agreement was made between Sanliurfa and Hasakah province in 1999. With special permission, relatives could pass over to the opposite country during the eids. Instead of news of greeting each other tearfully from behind barbed wire fences, there were now joyful scenes of those who had passed into the other country. Of course, I'm not counting the war era, but how is it that aunt Zehra couldn't come to Turkey while she had a such a blatant opportunity. I no longer doubted that her father was a heartless bastard, but was her husband just as insolent as well? Couldn't he be so kind as to bring this woman to the border the least for the eid? I asked aunt Zehra why she didn't come to the border during eids. I didn't add her husband to my question, as I didn't want her to get upset. However, aunt Zehra replied as though she read my inner thoughts.

"My husband was a very good man, Allah rest his soul, but he never brought up the subject of the border nor going back to the country. I remember the year border visits began as if it was yesterday. I was inside watching the news on the television while my husband was sitting on the porch with Hifza. This news was being read and I turned up the volume of the television so loud that the entire street heard the news. My husband was the only one who didn't hear it, I guess he pretended not to hear it. I was deploring him with my steely look. He didn't give a care in the world. Like his cousin's wife, perhaps he was afraid that I'd never come back if I went to

Turkey. I was afraid that everything would be ruined between us if I said what was on my mind."

_I'm very sad, aunt Zehra. I'm sad that I made you sad and that all this had made you sad. If only you were able to come back.

_I couldn't come, Yusuf, I told you, I was in a serious bind. But here I am now, and do you know why?

_I know, aunt Zehra. You escaped death. Anyone else would've done the same. Thank Allah you were able to get here safe and sound.

_You're right, son, we came to Turkey wanting a life in which we'll die of old age instead by a bullet. But the real reason was not to flee death, son. There are things worse than death. I came here as I feared that my daughter and I were going to become spoils of war.

_Spoils of war, how's that possible?

_Son, women and girls are spoils of war during wartime. In fact, you're the easiest war booty if your husband is died or if you're an orphan girl. They'll nab you and sell you from hand to hand and make you their slave. I came here so they wouldn't take my daughter from me.

Having remained silent since the moment we sat at the table, Hifza grabbed her mother's hand impulsively. She still didn't say a word, but she spoke with her eyes. You needed to be heartless not to comprehend that her sidewise slanting head and sad facial expression said, *"Be quiet, please don't say anymore!"* Aunt Zehra went silent and I went silent too, after Hifza's intervention. For awhile, only the teaspoons and forks were making sounds at the table. I looked in the faces of mother and my brothers without them noticing. They were all sad. Even my brother Muhsin, whom I believed didn't bear any other sense other than the five basic senses, was going to cry if I touched him. I was really upset with myself. It was unconscionable to question this mother and daughter who experienced suffering of the type none of us at this table could even imagine, and I did exactly that. It was about time I stashed my curiosity in a corner. Asking what happened to Hifza and why she didn't want her mother to speak would be good only for stabbing an open wound. I decided to wait for the day Hifza would tell her story herself. Then again, I couldn't remain silent. I needed to blow life into a table that was suffocating in mourning. And I knew exactly how do to this.

The moment I said, *"You have a fabulous star, Aunt Zehra. You look absolutely marvelous,"* everyone looked at me, then over to aunt Zehra. While aunt Zehra *"Thank you, son,"* I couldn't tell how happy that sweet smile that appeared on her face made me. I was like a sinner whose repentance was accepted. It was as if the dark clouds looming over the table had dissipated with aunt Zehra's smile. I now needed to make another gesture that would bring out the sun. I started telling about Anita. I told of her smile, her tattoos, her sympathic state of mind and her friendliness to the extent that I was sure everyone at that table thought I was in love with Anita. In saying Anita was thirty years old, I averted any misunderstandings. My actual intent was to send Hifza a message, and I really didn't care what the others were thinking.

After telling about Anita and her interpreter friend Sevda in all their regalia, I turned back to aunt Zehra in askance, *"Can I introduce you to Anita? You can tell her about your star."* I needed to keep my promise I made to Anita and I was going to conveniently handle the situation if I could only convince aunt Zehra. At least I wouldn't have to go all the way to Sanliurfa to find a relative that had a tattoo. Aunt Zehra didn't disappoint me, saying with that sweet smile of hers, *"Sure, son, as you wish."*

Although we were unable to reach a conclusion about the ID crisis, we got up joyfully from the breakfast table that I had drowned in melancholy. None of us knew what would emerge from the coming days, and we were like family members who had reunited years later. I wanted very much to stay longer in this endearing environment, but I also had to go to work. It was 8:30 AM and I was going to be three hours late when I arrived at the shop. Anyways, mother rang Hayri before we sat down at breakfast and told him I was going to be late today. *Dangalak* Hayri was forced to find another reason to bitch at me today. I didn't care what he said, I was going to wait for the day to end without him ruining the excitement I had inside me.

Anyways, I had no energy to deal with *dangalak* Hayri's bullshit. My mind was on Anita. Before leaving home, I whatsapped Sevda, saying, *"If you're free, let's meet at the same café tomorrow afternoon. I have someone to introduce to Anita."* Sevda replied immediately, as if she had been expecting my message all along. I smiled when I read her answer she emojied with smiles, *"Great, I'll talk with Anita and write you back."*

I had never left home with a smile on my face, even on a workday. I thought about this while I put on my shoes. Boy did I go through a lot of emotional changes in such a short period of time. I was afraid, I was angry, I smiled, I was happy. I went out the door hoping my happiness wouldn't be ruined. I saw mother and my brother in front of the door. My brother Yahya looked like he was caught redhanded with his hand in the cookie jar as he averted his glance towards at the ground. Having not spoken a word during breakfast, I wondered why Yahya was holding mother prisoner in front of the door. I asked mother, *"What's going on?"* My brother cut in before mother had a chance to open her mouth, *"What do you mean, what's going on, it's what's going to happen, can't you see, Yusuf? This woman's going to burn our family. What if she files a complaint against mom, or claims all of dad's property for herself? I mean, she's dad's official wife!"*

I understood my brother's reticence, and this reaction of his didn't surprise me. Despite the fact he never had any problems in his life, or any love-fraught headaches, he always prepared worst-case scenarios for himself. It was perhaps for this reason that he lead an enviously peaceful and organized life. Which is exactly why he was such a bore. He sat there with all his boredom throughout breakfast. It was clear he was playing chess in his mind again, calculating his worse-case scenarios. I had no ready reply for my brother's query. What was really going to happen from now on? I looked in mother's face. From what I gathered, she had no answer in her head, but at least she wasn't as pessimistic as my brother. She was calm as usual. She knew how to douse a fire well. In fact, not only fire, but knew well how to pour water on those who enflamed the fire. If just temporarily, mother knew to extinguish the fire burning inside my brother Yahya, saying, *"Don't think bad thoughts, son. Let's let some time pass, everything will be fine. Just cut the poor woman some slack. Keep in mind that whatever I am, aunt Zehra is the same, as well. She's okay with us, if she wants to stay here. Besides, we owe a debt of gratitude to both her and her daughter. Don't fret about the property or whatnot. Zehra is not the kind of woman who makes a big deal about such matters."*

From: Hifza
Subject: ***Whatever happens, I'm not going to die!***
Sept 10th, 2014

Nearly a month had passed since we had gathered at the breakfast table to listen to the stories of both mother and aunt Meryem. The ID situation hadn't been brought up even once since then. Everyone pretty much left the sleeping dogs lie. Mother and I had practically become a part of this family. There was nary a trace of our first day worries. In fact, the neighbors knew mother as Yusuf's aunt who'd come from Syria, which left me as Yusuf's cousin. Everyone with the exception of Yusuf played along with this game. While Yusuf may have accepted mother as his aunt, he didn't consider me as his cousin.

Actually, he didn't want to have such consideration. He opposed even the presumption of such a family tie. He was thinking such ties between us needed to be as distant as possible. I was the daughter of the daughter of his father's uncle. Even this link bothered Yusuf, but at least a link of this distance was a situation that he could stomach. Because he loved and he didn't possess the fortitude that could identify with the idea of falling in love with a girl who was a close relative. So, that's the reason he didn't want anyone to know, not even himself, that we were relatives, even if we were distant relatives. I was even more cautious than Yusuf. I wasn't even thinking about the relative connection. I was a young girl whose future was still unclear and was only thinking there was no place for love in my life at the moment. Then again, I also didn't want to lose Yusuf.

Actually, I despised Yusuf when I first saw him. I especially hated Yusuf the day we were discussing the ID situation over breakfast. His attitude as he interrogated mother upset me to no end. The way he behaved, as though we had come to steal something from their lives, really got on my nerves. When in fact, his father had stolen something from us. Something important enough to keep us going in life. Yusuf ignored this reality and was firing off questions as if he was a police detective who had caught a petty burglar. I found his behavior repulsive. However, once I got to know Yusuf a little, I understood he bore evil intent, and that he was a kind person, the likes of which are rarely encountered in this world of ours. In fact, I understood later on that I was the only reason for him spewing strange sentences and nonsense from time to time at that breakfast table.

All his excitement of looking at me while saying he was going to introduce mother to Anita rendered him incapable of forming proper sentences. I laughed for a long time when I learned this. In fact, without realizing it, I laughed so loud that mother, who was sitting a few tables away from us, broke away from the conversation she was having with Anita and Sevda and looked at our table. Once mother gestured with her head as to mean, *"What's going on?"* I leaned my head to the ground in embarrassment. Then I told Yusuf it would be better if we went to the table where our mothers were sitting.

We picked up our chairs and went over to our mothers' table. The discussion of topic at the table was the star tattoo on mother's chin. Anita asked questions, Sevda translated and mother told her story. Anita was jotting down every sentence she heard. Once in a while, she'd look my way and smile. After finishing her conversation with mother, she turned to me and asked, *"Why don't you have a tattoo?"* I told her that while I liked the star on mother's chin, I never thought to have a tattoo made up for myself. Anita said grinningly, *"Perhaps you'll consider one in the future. You have a beautiful face, a tattoo would look just as well on you as it does your mother."* I smiled too as I looked at Sevda and said, *"Anyways, if I were to have a tattoo done up, I'd do it only because it looks good, but I'm not going to have any mark etched anywhere on my body to have a good fortune."* The moment Sevda finished her translation, Anita asked one more question with a surprised expression on her face. She wanted to know if I believed the meaning of the star on mother's chin. My reply was a single word. *"No."*

My single word reply was so harsh that Anita was dumbfounded. This reaction of mine must have struck such a nerve with Anita that she opened a fresh page for me and was jotting down everything I said. I didn't understand what she wrote in her notebook as she wrote in English. For all I knew, she might be writing that I was one of those degenerated youths who didn't want to become a part of a deep-rooted culture. In fact, I wasn't rejecting my own culture. I was only against meanings that were conveyed into tattoos belonging to our own culture and I didn't believe that these tattoos would bring their owners any luck.

Anita asked why I felt so negative about tattoos. I gestured with my head towards mother, saying the reason for my thinking was sitting right across from her. *"Grandma etched that star into mother's chin so it would bring her good fortune. You listened to mother's story, now answer me this question. Do you think it has brought mother good luck? I also don't believe that we're going to be lucky."* Listening intently to the translation of my words, Anita held my hand with a sad look on her face and said I was right. Then she told me something I would never forget: *"You're right Hifza, you know what? Tattoos don't really bring their owners luck but rather tattoos remind them of their duty. Some tattoos remind them they need to pull themselves together and hang in there at their weakest, most susceptible moment. Some remind them they are loved, while others remind them they need to keep their distance. You can refresh yourself in every curve of the tattoo and rejuvenate your hope in every line. What tattoos remind you only bring you a good fortune, not their mystical power. You create your own fortune."*

I grasped Anita's hand tightly and said that I could have a tattoo done after this down-to-earth explanation of hers. But I told her I wanted to have a tattoo etched onto my body from where she came. I explained that I preferred this as a tattoo from my own lands would remind me of nothing but pain and suffering. Once mother also said it was okay, I gave my word to Anita. I was going to have one of the tattoos etched on my body that Anita recommended as soon as we settled down with Mother. Maybe I could have tattoos done on the side of my eyes, like Anita. My eyes were the window from where I looked at the world and I would've liked to be reminded of my father and brother on the edge of my window.

Meeting Anita and Sevda was a wonderful experience to talk about the meaning of tattoos. I can't describe the feeling of wearing the new dress and shoes Aunt Meryem and I bought together, of walking about Istanbul without the fear of being killed, and the taste of drinking coffee in a nice café. However, for me, the most important thing was to get to know Yusuf even better. I was really impressed by his slow manner of speaking, so I'd understand everything perfectly and the way he repeated some words without getting fed up, just so I'd learn them. I was amazed by his kindness and gentle attitude. I began to feel intimate towards him and no longer felt embarrassed by sitting slant-wise across from him. Yusuf also looked like he didn't care about the way I sat. Though my pain, which was the reason for my sitting at an angle, steadily increased, Yusuf's indifference put me at ease. However, it was time to find a solution to this pain of mine.

The ointment that mother got from an old lady back in Hasakah had run out a long time ago. It didn't do me any good anyways. Realizing that my pain was sometimes too unbearable, mother said it was about time to get some help from aunt Meryem. She thought aunt Meryem take me to a hospital for treatment. I thought the same, but I was embarrassed. The source of my pain wasn't my arm or my leg. I also had a story which was the reason for my pain and, I didn't want anyone else to know this Allahdamned story. That's why I said insistingly to mother, *"Let's just you and I go to a doctor, nobody else has to know."* This is why mother was waiting for the right time to cash in her gold chain she hid in her breast so she could take me to the hospital.

Thanks to Yusuf, mother no longer needed to cash in her gold chain and keep me waiting in this excruciating pain.

It was the evening of the last day of August 2014, mother and aunt Meryem were visiting a neighbor. For some reason, Muhsin, who never seemed to emerge from his room, wasn't at home either. Yusuf and I were alone. We were having fun spending time together, drinking tea and watching TV, making fun of the Mafioso character in the series that was on. We LOL'led while he taught me words to improve my Turkish. Then we got closer, close enough to feel the heat of our skin. I was enjoying this feeling for the first time. I was trying to keep maintain my distance on one hand, while I also wanted to flitter about on Yusuf's warm skin like a butterfly that wanted to spice up its brief lifespan. When he held my hand and placed a little kiss on my neck as much as my headscarf allowed, I let myself go in Yusuf's arms.

There was nothing else I could do the moment I felt his warm breath on my neck. I was no longer leaning against the edge of the armchair, but rather against Yusuf's trustworthy body. Everything was really different when the hand caressing my body belonged to someone I loved. I couldn't describe the pleasure I experienced while Yusuf's hand wandered over my body like a warm, sweet breeze. I was happy, I was calm and I didn't even want to think about the consequences. Because I trusted Yusuf. However, even that trust couldn't get me to forget about the trauma in the depths of my soul.

When I felt the hand that I let caress my breasts, the piece of cloud I first stretched out in pleasure on my belly then on my abdomen turned into a bed of nails. Suddenly, I let out a horrific scream. I impulsively pulled back. I was no longer in the arms I trusted very much. I leaned onto the other side of the armchair and went into a crying fit. I can't explain the shame and fear I saw on Yusuf's face. I was going to put Yusuf at ease if I could only extricate myself from my fit of crying. I was going to say, "You're not the cause of my scream and my tears," but I couldn't stop myself for some reason. I was getting worse the more Yusuf apologized and it was as if I was going to pass out from hiccupping. Despite all his embarrassment, Yusuf acted with aplomb by picking me up and carrying me into the bathroom. He opened the spigot and washed my hands and face. When I lifted my head and looked in the mirror, I saw the embarrassment on Yusuf's face once more. I managed to smile as tears ran from down my cheeks as we made eye contact. I was drifting on the edge like a schizophrenic. I relaxed a bit when Yusuf also smiled. This time, I splashed water on my own face, stood up suddenly and hugged Yusuf, who was waiting at my side. His face, neck and T-shirt were drenched.

I was trembling on my feet as if I was having a epilepsy seizure. Yusuf said, *"I'm sorry, I think I went too far."* I just said, *"Be quiet"* as I continued to give him a shivering embrace. My wet lips made contact with Yusuf's lips. I was kissing someone on the lips for the first time. If only all the firsts I experiences were as incredible as the one I experienced that moment. I thought to myself, *"He has to know everything"* as I enjoyed the pleasure that descended from Yusuf's lips to my heart. With a swift movement, I broke away from Yusuf's arms, and I said *"There are some things I need to tell you about my past."* His reflection was really encouraging. *"You don't have to tell me anything about your past, Hifza. If it's going to make you feel better, sure, you can tell me. But know that whatever happened to you, whatever you experienced in those fields of death, would be interesting to me only to give you support."* he said.

Yusuf had a character that left no doubt as to what he meant to say while he spoke. No innuendo ever left his mouth. He spoke concisely and to the point. He said, he loved me without beating around the bush only increased my admiration for him. I could sustain a life far from hypocrisy and lies with someone who even expressed his fondness for me so plainly. However, that moment, I had to postpone this dream a little more. Regardless of how much Yusuf says *"You don't have to explain,"* he had the right to know about my past and I couldn't perceive what kind of reaction he would have when he heard what I was going to tell him. I didn't know if this love that bloomed so shortly was going to disappear into nothingness. I had to risk this foreboding conclusion. I couldn't be unfair to Yusuf. I had to be at least as honest as him. I also told him what was on my mind when he handed me a clean towel to dry my hands and face. I told him, *"I haven't told anybody the things I'm going to tell you except my mother. In fact, my mother doesn't even know some of the things I'm going to tell you. But I'm not going to keep anything from you. Because you deserve this."*

Yusuf didn't say anything, but just smiled and caressed my moist cheek with the back of his hand like he did whenever we were alone. I wanted to kiss his fingers that wandered over my cheek. I was shy, and said to myself, *wait!* I grasped the handly tightly I wanted to kiss, then dragged Yusuf behind me as far as the living room. I hand him sit in the armchair and leaned his back into the armchair. He was like a doll with moving limbs in my hands. I took a chair from the dining table and sat opposite him. I said, *"Now I'm going to tell you about the days I want to forget. Please don't interrupt what I have to say even once. Don't even ask any questions. I want to tell you and get it out of the way already, without any shame and without holding back all at once."* As I knew Yusuf had an emotional character, I knew it would open some deep wounds in his heart. I also knew that there would be nothing we could share in this life if he couldn't share in my pain. Which is why I took a deep breath and began to tell my story. I want to tell not only to Yusuf, but like my voice wanted to inform all of humanity from a podium set up on a mountaintop.

Everyone was thrilled when the Arab Spring also called on our country four years ago. Everyone poured into the streets. The crowds were hurling slogans at Bashar in great excitement and dancing the local 'dabke' dance.

Your legitimacy here has ended
Get out Bashar
We will remove Bashar with our strength
Syria wants freedom'

Instead of the regular tongue-twisters, this hit song was on everyone's lips. Even the kids in the street were having a blast belting out this tune. According to what the elders were saying, the winds of freedom were inevitably going to blow in Syria as well, and like Tunisia and Egypt, the dictator in our country was going to be tossed out, the tyranny was going to end and we were going to be happier. I was still a child, I had no idea, but they didn't know that the thing they thought was the wind of freedom would soon turn into a storm of death in Syria. Once the songs of freedom went silent and the weapons started talking, everyone, including us children understood that the enthusiastic winds we thought was spring was in reality, the storm of death. This was the storm that was brought on either wittingly or unwittingly by the people who poured into the streets, thinking they were going to bring on the spring. They amassed in tempo and harmony as they sang their songs on the street thinking it would be enough to topple the regime. It wasn't long before those who hurled "Down with Assad" slogans in unison started shooting at each other. Everyone wanted the spring to come only to their neighborhood. Do you think spring would come to such a country! Anyways, it never came. Guns and bombs from other countries came instead of spring. With these weapons came monsters who committed massacres. Rapists and plunderers came too as part of the bargain.

Things got so bad that we couldn't go out into the streets and go to school. We couldn't get bread from the bakery whenever we wanted and couldn't find any food in the shops or markets. In fact, it got to the point we couldn't even find shops or markets most of the time. While all this was happening, we were still a family that grinned and bore all the tribulations at home. We were all together and loved each other very much. We were of the firm belief that these troubling days would end sooner or later. The storm of death that came disguised as the spring still hadn't stolen the smiles from our faces. Of course, everything has an end, and that also meant our smiles. My father gave his life beneath bombs while buying bread from the bakery six months ago, and my brother who was with him, is still missing. I still don't know who committed this monstrosity or why they did it. But I do know that my father's death killed our spirit. The smile on our face disappeared forever along with my brother. Our house was a house of mourning. Our days passed searching for my brother and our nights passed in rivers of tears. All this, as we prayed, we wouldn't be subject to our worst fears. What more could we be afraid of; our father was dead and, my brother had disappeared. What worse could happen!

With the fading out of the last smile, mother and I both knew very well we weren't the imaginary heroines of any movie or book. We also realized that the possibility of an experience that would haunt us in which we would prefer to die rather than to live would be higher than the possibility of us staying alive. The thing that frightened us the most after my father's death or my brother's disappearance was certainly not death, but rather falling into the hands of ISIS. It was the end of February 2014, and ISIS had yet to assault Hasakah. But the danger wasn't faraway. Like everyone else, we all knew what had happened to the Yazidi women and children in Iraq. Non-Muslim women and children were war spoils for ISIS. They nabbed women and children of all ages, sold them, used them as slaves and raped them until they got bored, then presented them to other rapists.

As ISIS gained territory in Syria, the slave markets where they sold women and children and the rape chambers were also spreading in waves to our country. Of course we were Moslem, but we knew that our being Moslem wasn't going to change anything. If we fell into the hands of ISIS, it was inevitable we were to be taken to be sold and used as sex slaves. That's because there were no men in our homes.

We were getting news about the regions captured by ISIS. We heard they had opened guest houses called *madd-afe* for Muslim women who didn't have menfolk in their homes. It would be wrong to call them *guest houses*. These were another slave market for ISIS men. Women and girls who were imprisoned in these homes because they didn't have any males in their household were forced to marry ISIS fighters. The way that covered the religious aspect of acquiring sex slaves from amongst Muslim women and girls passed through these houses. Well, this was the experience we were going to prefer death instead. Imprisoned in the maddafe and forced to marry with our rapist would've been a situation worse than death. Worse than that would be not knowing who the rapist would sell us to when he got bored. We spoke with mother as to what we should do in the face of such a situation. If we encountered this situation, we were going to say we were in the guardianship of one of father's relatives. We were forced to make such a choice as all of mother's relatives were in Turkey. We thought uncle Ubeyd would protect us if necessary by saying he was engaged to either. But the blow we expected from ISIS came from the uncle whom we believed would be our guardian.

Uncle Ubeyd dropped by almost every day after father's death. He would occasionally bring some food with him. Most days, we would go out looking for my brother Ahmed and I thought that Uncle Ubeyd was such a nice person compared to our other relatives. I prayed that he would be with us all the time. It was the morning of a night I had prayed for him again that Uncle Ubeyd knocked on our door. He said breathlessly, *"Hifza, get ready, I heard that Ahmed may be in a house that could be treating his injuries, let's go and see if he's there."*

Mother said, "I'm coming too," as she worriedly started putting her shoes on. However, my uncle said only two people could ride on his motorcycle. He grabbed Mother's arm and dragged her back inside, saying, *"You stay here. You do what I tell you, do you want to go there and faint in the middle of a bunch of wounded people?"* Then he turned and gave me a stern look, shouting, *"Get your shoes on, we're going to that house."* From that point, there was nothing left that neither my mother nor I could do. Though his manner was stern, in the end we were facing a good-hearted uncle who thought that mother would be adversely affected by the wounded.

I sat sidewise on the motorbike as I hugged my uncle tightly so I wouldn't fall off. I affixed myself to my uncle's back as his fat belly didn't let me clasp my hands together. The weather was so hot that despite the wind that whipped our faces, my uncle's belly began to sweat. As if sticking to his belly fat like a baby rhesus monkey so I wouldn't fall off wasn't enough, I was forced to put up with his sweat getting my hands all wet. I began getting anxious when I was quite some distance from home and asked him where we were going. I repeated my question a few times as he couldn't hear above the noise of the motorcycle. I could only hear him say, *"We're almost there, my girl. Hang in there."* After my uncle said that, we travelled even that much further. There were no longer any houses or people around us. We were proceeded over a bumpy dirt road. Hasakah was way behind us by then.

I thought that perhaps the home we were headed towards was a secret hospital. After all, we were living in a country where the hospitals were getting bombed. At any rate, my fears began to increase the further away we got away from Hasakah. I hugged my uncle even tighter without worrying about his sweaty stench. I was on this noisy motorcycle that shook up all my internal organs for nearly an hour and I was exhausted. Just when I was going to ask my uncle, *"How much further do we have?"*, we stopped in front of a house with a garden on the side of the road. I said to myself, *"Alhamdulillah, what a relief!"* when the earsplitting noise of the motorcycle went silent. My uncle lowered the kickstand and told me to wait. I didn't say a word even though I was scared of staying alone. I thought there was no way he would leave me outside and go into the house. There were no other houses around, let alone any trees, we were in the middle of the steppes.

When my uncle reached the garden gate a few meters ahead, he yelled out, *"Peace be with you brother, where are you hadji?"* Meanwhile, I was looking at a wall high enough to conceal the house in the garden from the outside. I figured they erected such a high wall to protect the house they built as a hospital from attack. That moment, the wall appeared to have disintegrated in front of my eyes and thought the wall they pulled father's torn up body from beneath was as least as thick as this one. What a bummer it couldn't protect my father. I wanted to scream out the revolt that swelled up inside me to the elders behind this wall.

I wanted to say *"What good is this wall standing the height of five men when there are winged killers in the air! You provoke the winged killers and called them to the top of our homes. While you're eating each other below, you're killing us from above. Are you happy now?"* It was all on the tip of my tongue. However, it was neither the time nor the place to expound upon my rebellion. *"What do I care about the wall now, I hope my brother is inside and we can get him out of there. Dear Allah, I'm begging you to help us!"* I began to pray. The garden gate finally opened while I was praying. My uncle embraced a man who was older than my father, and he began mumbling about something, rambling on for what seemed to be an eternity. As for me, I was on the verge of collapsing into a heap from anxiety at the foot of the motorcycle. I didn't have the nerve to ask, *"C'mon uncle, what are we waiting for?"* I couldn't disrespect a male who was an family elder even in that situation.

The bearded man with a turban wrapped around his head talking with my uncle had a weapon practically a mile-long hanging from his back. My guess was that the doctors and patients inside were protected with this gun. I realized that the man who carried this giant weapon on his back with the barrel pointed at the ground was looking at me every so often. He was looking at me after every word he said to uncle Ubeyd. I turned my back and began waiting. This time, I began worrying about what was going on. Because they were whispering, and I couldn't hear what they were saying. I could endure it no longer and turned back to see them shaking hands. While muttering to myself, *"What, you couldn't find a better time to chat?"* the strangeness on my uncle's face caught my attention. My uncle was tense, and he had an anxious countenance.

I was trying to figure out what was going on when the armed man took out a bundle of money from his pocket and handed it to my uncle. I was sure I was now confronted with a terrible situation when my uncle bid the armed man farewell and started walking my way with the same facial expression. My uncle's strangeness on his face and his coming back without going in riveted two worse case situations into my mind like nails. My brother wasn't inside. Perhaps even worse was that the armed guy told my uncle that my brother was dead. At that brief moment, I hoped that the second possibility had come true. I was furious at myself for thinking such thoughts. To be honest, mother and I were totally exhausted from all this uncertainty. Perhaps that exhaustion was the reason I couldn't think straight, I don't know. Whatever the case, I didn't have the time to make that assertion, and I couldn't think later on.

My uncle didn't look in my face until he came up next to me. I could no longer hold back as I ask him what was going on. He didn't reply as he got on his bike. I shouted, *"Uncle, what's happening? Answer me, did something bad happen?"* Uncle still didn't utter a single word as he started up his machine. I stuck to his arm, saying, *"I'm not going anywhere until you answer me."* How stupid I was! Because I was still thinking my uncle was behaving like that because he got bad news about my brother. I was still assuming my uncle was a kind-hearted person. When in fact, I should have seen the warning sign when he took the handful of money from the guy with the gun. That moment, I indelibly etched the most pathetic side of the mind always defeated by optimism into my head through painful, bloody experience.

My feet left the ground suddenly when my uncle suddenly throttled up the bike with his right hand. Then I began to drag along the ground below the waist. I tried to hang on for dear life while shouting, *"What are you doing uncle, stopppp uncle, stopppp for Allah's sake!"* I was dragged in this manner for fifteen meters or so. The fiend didn't even look at me once. Then he accelerated so quickly, I no longer had the strength to hang on. While falling away from the motorcycle, I hit my head on the metal foot rest. I rolled onto the ground as the motorcycle hurtled on. My legs, hands and face were a bloody mess. Soil that got onto my black abaya mixed with the blood to turn into mud.

I couldn't even cry out of astonishment. My uncle with

whom we thought to take shelter when ISIS arrived had sold me down the river. He left me in the middle of nowhere and went off. I had no idea what was in store for me. I didn't know the armed man who paid off my uncle, and I didn't know what sort of hell this high-walled enclave was. I was beaten but I tried to pull myself together, knowing that I had to get away from there. I tried to straighten up on my bloody hands as if I was leaving fingerprints on a dirt road. Just as I was getting to my feet over my knees, someone grabbed my right arm from behind. Out of fear, I turned my head and looked to my right. I came eye-to-eye with the armed guy who gave my uncle money. That's the moment I started crying. I wanted one of the bombs that killed my father to fall on me right then and there. I lost feeling in my feet out of both fear and pain. I couldn't feel any part of myself and couldn't see anything as well. Even the sun overhead had darkened, I thought I was dying and, I recited myself the last rites, *"Ashadu an la ilaha illallah wa ashadu anna Muhammadan abduhu wa Rasuluhu."*

I woke up with a scent that seeped into my nose. There was an old lady over me when I opened my eyes. She was rubbing an onion on my nose with her hand. I wanted to leap from where I was, but I had no strength to move my arm. I was paralyzed and could only move my head. The onion in the woman's hand was still next to my nose. I had the strength to say just a couple of words and I didn't want to expend it to say, *"Take that onion away from my nose."* I looked at the old woman's eyes and asked her, *"What are you going to do with me?"* while feeling my tears trickling towards my ears. She got up from my side, saying, *"Be quiet, you didn't die."* She went out of the room with the onion in her hand. While looking behind her, I tried to comprehend where I was. There was a carpet in the middle, cushions along the edges of the walls, a pile of white cloth in the opposite corner, a window covered with a cloth that served in lieu of a curtain, and a naked lightbulb in the ceiling. Next to me were a bowl of water, tubes of ointment and blood-stained cloths. I looked at my arms which had a yellow ointment spread on them. I exerted my last ounce of energy to lift my head and look at my feet. My wounds were covered in the same color pomade. I tired even as I blinked my eyes. I feel asleep.

When I awoke, the naked bulb in the ceiling was emitting a yellow light. I wasn't alone in the room. The woman who pressed the onion onto my nose was sitting at the foot of the opposite wall. She got up from where she sat, saying, *"C'mon, sit up, I'm going to bring you some soup."* I lifted my head off the pillow, cautiously straightening up as I leaned my back against the wall. I lifted my leg the moment I found the strength in me to get to my feet and walk. Realizing I was getting up, the old woman turned around and tried to have me sit on a cushion. I screamed at the top of my lungs, *"Leave me alone, I'm going to go home."* I felt the deep abrasions in my face bleed due to the tense movements of my lips.

I tried to break free from the woman's arms. She grabbed me so tight that I even felt the calluses on her hands through my dress. While trying desperately to free myself from the woman, the bearded filth who paid off my uncle came in screaming. This time, the gun was in his hands. He slapped my face hard while I was struggling to break free of the old woman's arms. My eyes suddenly darkened. I sat back down on the cushion that I was just laying on without the old woman forcing me to do so. The gun barrel was at the tip of my nose. His hoarse threats of "Sit back down in your place and worry about getting well. Otherwise I'll empty the magazine in your head and toss your body into the dump out back" were ringing in my ears. While death was at the tip of my nose, I thought of mother. After my brother, the poor woman was now without me… I could only say, *"May Allah damn you, Uncle Ubeyd."* My tears were no longer trickling remorsely as I began to sob.

While I cried, I thought it was time to make a decision. I either had to die quickly or else I had to find a way out of here. As I didn't experience a problem until that moment that deemed I had to die, I decided to find a way to free myself from this high-walled hell. I had to accomplish this for both me and for my mother. As I knew that I wouldn't be saved without recuperating and without being strong enough to be able to at least run outside the house. So, I ate all of the soup the old lady brought me. I finished the bread on the side without leaving so much as a crumb. Then I laid down.

Surprised to see me finish the soup in calm fashion, the old woman didn't say anything. She picked up the soup bowl and went outside. She had a glass of tea when she returned. I thought she had brought the tea for me. Just as I was sitting up in my place, the woman sat back down at the foot of the opposite wall. While sipping her tea, she began cutting the white cloth in the corner of the wall in specific sizes. She was folding and stacking the long pieces she cut. I was wondering what the white cloths were good for, but I was still thinking about the tea. I closed my eyes, saying *"Drink poison you old witch!"* My plan was clear. I was going to recuperate and find a way to beat these two old fuckers.

I was awakened by a noise that came from the floor of

the room. It wasn't completely light outside as I looked toward the window. I saw the old lady when I turned my head to the right. She was donning a white headscarf and was doing her obligatory prayers with her black abaya. Prostrating herself, she placed her knees in such a position, the sound was as though she was striking concrete with a sledgehammer. I could tell she was conducting the morning prayer from the number of rakats. It was almost dawn. The question of whether I'd be able to see another sunrise had crossed my mind. Never mind what would happen to me, I didn't even know who this old lady and the armed guy were. I looked back at the old woman. She had finished her prayers and was praying with her hands in the air. As if she was able to read my mind if I looked straight at her, I averted my glance up to the ceiling. I muttered to myself, *"Are you begging for forgiveness for all the evil you did to me, bitch? You think Allah is going to accept your praying!"*

I began waiting, thinking she might sleep after her praying. If she slept, I was going to try to escape without making a sound. She didn't sleep but rather passed in front of me and sat down. Once again, she continued cutting the white cloth in the wall corner into certain sizes and stack them. While I pretended I was sleeping, realized the white rags she was piling on top of each other were not in the room the day before. I couldn't understand what anyone was using so many white rags for. The only possibility that came to mind was that they were sewing and selling thawb, which is ankle length dress worn by men. So, I guess there were people out there who could afford to buy so many white thawbs at a time when even buying a loaf of bread was nearly impossible. I was unable to pretend sleeping long enough to ponder this situation as the chagrin in my body didn't allow me to remain alert.

I saw mother in my dream. I was sitting between her legs, leaning against her chest, just like I did when I was a child. She was embracing me from behind, holding my hands and whispering into my ear, "I have your fear in my hands," just like she did when I was a child. My mommy would do the same thing whenever I was afraid during my childhood. She would cover me up and transform into an armored shield that kept evil away from me. I actually believed that mother took the fear out of me when she held my hands tightly and whispered, "I have your fear in my hands." I no longer cared about whatever frightened me, whether it was the darkness, a noise or whatnot. I felt refreshed. I didn't feel the same refreshment when I opened my eyes. Because my hand was in the hand of the old woman who was the source of my fears. She was telling me, *"Get up already!"* Her face was so close to mine that her beard sprouting from a mole on her chin was touching my cheek. Startled and disgusted, I straightened up in my place. Freeing my hand from the old woman as I retreated where I sat, I asked her, *"What do you want from me? Why did my uncle leave me in this house?"*

The old woman got to her feet and turning her back, her voice was stern, *"Hurry, get up, don't talk, you're going to take a bath now."* When I yelled, *"I'm not going to take any bath, I want to go home,"* the old woman, who was heading for the door, whipped back around. While she sauntered back over to me, I thought she was going to whoop me one. Bracing myself for the imminent blows, I pushed my head onto the cushion, got my arms around my head and gathered my legs to my chest. What I guessed did not transpire. The old woman grabbed my arm and made me stand up. She dragged me out of the room without a word. She forced me to walk to a door at the end of a narrow corridor. She opened the door and pushed me inside, saying, *"Your clothes are in the basket, your towel is hanging behind the door. There's a nail clipper and comb in front of the mirror. Cut your nails, wash up, comb your hair, and yell for me when you finish up. I'll come and open the door."* She tossed me inside like she was throwing out the garbage, then closed and locked the door behind me.

I was in the middle of both the bathroom and uncertainty. I sat down but didn't cry. I also didn't look for a window to escape from. They weren't as bird-brained as to lock me in a bathroom with a window I could flee from. I said to myself the best thing to end this uncertainty without further ado would be to take a bath and get out of the bathroom. But first I wanted to look at myself in the mirror. The lines on my faces had scabbed up. I removed my headscarf and gropingly felt around for the scars on my head. When I undressed, I saw bruises over almost my entire body. That's also when I noticed I was menstruating. I thought while my injuries on my body weren't enough, that I was going to struggle with menstruation pains. However, I thanked Allah when I perked my ears up to the voices coming from in front of the door. After listening to the conversation between the old woman and the armed guy that started off at a normal tone and turned into a verbal brawl, I understood why I was in that house.

The armed guy insisted that the old woman prepare me for that night. The old woman told him every time that I was injured and that he needed to wait a couple more days. When she said I wasn't going to enter the nuptial room in a wounded state, the armed man shouted, *"It's not her cunt that's wounded! Get her ready for tonight!"* Then the voices went silent. I went over to the door and collapsed at the foot in order to better hear their voices. Everything was quite apparent now. My uncle sold me to this man so I could be a second wife. I could no longer control my tears I resisted so they wouldn't flow.

I made another decision at the foot of the door. I said inwardly, *"It'll be better if I die rather than snuggling up with this guy."* I wasn't going to give in, but neither was I going to die. I made a plan for both contingencies. The first remedy that came to mind was to remove the scabby wounds on my face, but I believed this wouldn't stop the armed guy. For this reason, my first plan was to use my period. I knew that men who treated women like shit, treated those having their period even worse than shit and basically kept their distance from them. That's why my telling the old woman I was having my period who gain me time. What was I going to do if I couldn't extricate myself of that hell by the time my period ended in about a week's time? This is why I had to devise a plan. Because the bastard who screamed *"It's not her cunt that's wounded!"* was adamant he was going to rape me as soon as possible.

While all this was going through my mind, the large nailclippers in front of the mirror caught my attention. I then looked at my nails. They had grown long after I put off cutting them all this time. They had turned black, having filled with grit when I was dragged along the ground. I made my real plan while looking at my nails, knowing that I needed to have the nails on at least one of my hands long enough to carry out my plan.

I forced myself to get up from the floor where I sat. I calmly walked over to the mirror and gazed at myself in front of it for what seemed like an eternity. I talked with myself as I looked at my reflection. Staring at my injured face, I said, *"You don't have your mother at your side saying,* **'Your fear is in my hands'** *this time Hifza, you have to save yourself."* I picked up the nail clippers and started clipping my nails. I only clipped the nails on my right hand and dug out the crud under the nails on my left hand. I was going to hide my long nails by making a fist of my left hand. I knew that if I did the exact opposite that I'd have a tough time eating with my right hand.

The armed guy who wanted to rape me and the old woman whom I hadn't quite figured out the relationship she had with this bastard would definitely warn me not to be a non-believer by eating with my left hand. Then again, they would've clipped my long nails with their own hands so I wouldn't be a non-believer. After cutting my nails, I said three prayers while I was in the shower. The first was, *"Dear Allah, please have him back off from raping me because I'm having my period."* The second was, *"Dear Allah, let me find a way out of here during my period."* My third prayer was, *"Dear Allah, let him leave me when I use my nails."* In fact, even if I didn't believe it was going to happen a few times, I also prayed *"Dear Allah, let my uncle regret his actions and have him come back and take me back home."*

When I finished up in the bathroom, I knocked on the door as I didn't know the old woman's name. She unlocked the door as though she was waiting for me at the foot of the door. Even though I said inwardly, *"I hope she wasn't watching me through the peephole, I'm screwed if she noticed I didn't cut the nails on my left hand,"* my fear was for naught. She grabbed my arm and dragged me as far as the long room at the end of the corridor. As I was being dragged, I looked around carefully I order to get to know the house. We were passing through the middle of two dark-green walls. There were two room doors with no windows on my left side and a door on the right that was small and narrow, resembling a storage entrance, with a lock hanging from it. When we arrived at the door of the room I had been kept overnight, I saw the outer door they forced me inside at the end of the short corridor. I understood I was in a small house in the middle of huge walls. As no voices came from the other rooms, I was almost sure that only the old lady and the armed man were in the house.

When we entered the room, the old woman dragged me as far as the spot where I slept the night before, saying, *"Sit down, I'm going to bring your food."* Even before she turned her back, I told her I needed a clean rag. She stomped out of the room without even asking me, *"What do you need a rag for?"* She locked the door behind her. When she returned, she was holding my dirty headscarf I had tossed into the basket in the bathroom. *"I can't waste a clean rag on your dirty blood. I gave you a clean dress, isn't that enough? Take this and stick it between your legs,"* as she tossed my headscarf on me. She understood why I asked for a clean rag even though I didn't tell her I was having my period. I was stunned by this attitude showed by the old woman who didn't want me to sleep with the old man with all my injuries.

At first, I was worried my plan to use my period wasn't going to work. However, I relaxed a bit when the old lady asked me how long my period was going to last. I told her, *"It lasts at least a week."* She exited the room without saying anything again. I was all alone in a room filled with a pile of white rags in the corner. I looked at the headscarf in my hand. It had bloodstains from when my head struck the ground while being dragged behind the motor-cycle. Instead of cleaning the blood with blood, I coveted the white rags in the corner. Scared the old woman would come back, I got up quickly from my place. I took one of the rags in the corner that hadn't been cut and folded yet. With the pair of scissors lying there, I cut a piece a little smaller than half a meter square. I folded it up and stuck it immediately in my underwear, then returned lickety-split to my place. After sitting down, I also stuck my dirty head-scarf between my skirt and underwear.

The old woman returned while I was trying to straight-en the rag that was bothering me when I hurriedly stuck in my underwear. She said, *"Get up, as long as you are having your period, you're going in the room with the other women."* So, it appears there were others in the house besides the old woman and the armed man. I was in a real funk know-ing it would be tough trying to flee from a crowded house. In order for her not to grab me tightly by the arm and drag me around the place, I got to my feet myself. We proceed-ed, with me in front and her behind me. She wanted me to stop when we came in front of the second door in the corri-dor. Removing her keychain from the pocket of her abaya, I promptly got the answer to my question, *"Who are these other women?"* As they were kept behind a locked door, it seemed they, like myself, were also held here against their will. I toyed with the idea that maybe we could organize a joint getaway plan together. When the old woman opened the door and pushed me inside, I saw four women sitting at the foot of separate walls. The only items in the room were a carpet, and a water pitcher and glass in the opposite corner. The reason why the walls were dark green like the corridor was because the room was in darkness. Steel bars blocked the light coming from the window.

"I'm going to bring your food in a while. Those who want to go to the bathroom can go after the meal!" as the old woman locked the door behind me, there were four curious pairs of eyes looking at me and I eyed each of them in return. They were all middle-aged women with melancholy pouring down their faces. Their apparel struck my attention in that they were all the same. Long black skirts, long-sleeved brown cotton shirts, white headscarves... I was now a hundred per cent sure these women shared the same fate as me. Then again, while they didn't bear any visible scars, their appearance bellowed out their inner wounds.

A young woman with a nose ring in her thirties was sitting on the cushion closest to the door. I slid over to her. Before I had a chance to say anything, she leaned over to my ear and whispered, *"Do not speak loudly, they're listening from behind the door."* I looked at the other women, who nodded their heads in unison, *"That's right,"* as if they all knew what had been whispered into my ear. I spoke in a hushed tone, firing off a series of consecutive questions into the ear of the woman with the nose ring, such as, *"What are you doing here? Why am I here? Who is this armed man, who is this old lady?"* The woman held my hand as she asked my name, where I was from and who were my relatives. I answered each of her questions in a low voice. In the meantime, the other women gathered around me. I didn't ask any of them the same question. Because what I really I wanted to learn was who was keeping us there, and in particular, the identity of the armed man who wanted to rape me.

The woman with the nose ring asked me, *"Have you ever heard of Narmin the Shroud Lady?"* I said I had never heard of her. *"The old woman goes door to door in Hasakah, selling clothes and material. Her nickname is 'Narmin the Shroud Lady' as she sells shrouds. It's clear your mother also bought some stuff from this woman."* she said. I objected, saying, *"What does that have to do with anything?"*

I would've definitely known if this women had come to our house, and even if I'd forgotten everything, I would've remembered the humungous mole on her face and the hairs sprouting from it. Anyways, mother wasn't someone who shopped. Father would buy whatever was necessary and bring it home. When I said this, the woman with the nose ring insisted even if it wasn't mother, there was another relative who most definitely knew this woman. I was confused when she said, *"Otherwise, you wouldn't be here."* I said, *"What do you mean, just come out with it, for Allah's sake!"* as I grasped her hands. When they heard the key turn in the lock, the three women leapt back to their places like deers fleeing from their hunter. The woman with the nose ring broke away from my hand and gestured with her head for me to move away from her a bit.

The old woman appeared with a pot which she left the pot right in front of the doorway, then promptly went out, locking us in the room once more. The smutty woman sitting at the foot of the wall where the door was got up, picked up the pot and went over to the woman with the nose ring. We all gathered around the pot. We began eating the undercooked rice that had no oil and no salt with our hands. My left hand was still in a fist so my nails wouldn't show. Meanwhile, we continued to talk in hushed tones. The woman with the nose ring started off with, *"So let me guess, there are no men in your house, right?"* I said that my father was dead and my brother was lost, then I asked her how she knew we had no men at home. She replied with a bitter smile, *"The woman who imprisoned us here knows what goes on in the homes where she sells shrouds."* I insisted once again that the old woman didn't stop by our house. When she replied with, *"Even if your mother didn't make the purchase, someone else in your family most certainly bought your father's shroud from this woman,"* It slowly dawned on me what had happened. That's because my uncle handled all matters surrounding father's funeral.

I looked into the eyes of the woman with the nose ring, practically pleading with her, *"For Allah's sake, tell me what's going on here from start to finish."* The woman with the nose ring stared at me for a while after taking a lump of rice to her mouth that she made with her hand. I saw desperation in her eyes as she munched on the uncooked grains of rice. I swore to myself I was never going to fall into that desperate abyss. Furiously, I squeezed my left hand into an even tighter fist. My long nails hurt as they pierced my flesh. I enjoyed this experience. My nails were going to come in handy when the time came.

After swallowing the lump of rice in her mouth, the woman with the nose ring began to talk. Fearful Shroud Lady Narmin would come charging into the room at any moment, she began explaining everything that's going on as quickly and quietly as possible. In a jiffy, the woman with the nose ring said, *"That guy with the gun is Shroud Lady Narmin's husband, Waheed. He was a rogue, living like a total bum off the money his wife made. We heard that he went to Iraq last year. That's where he became a so-called mujahid."* Then she said Waheed had gone into Iraq without so much as a single hair on his face only to return to Hasakah about two months ago with a long beard, a gun on his back and lots of money in his pocket. According to what the woman was saying, whom I could easily understand her horrid disgust on her face every time she utters the name of Waheed, who has been chasing after every woman and child who hasn't men in their homes since the day he returned from Iraq. His wife Narmin knew how many women and children there were in homes where she sold a shroud. With the help of a father, a brother, a brother-in-law or another relative, Waheed bought the women his wife found and, he had them brought to this house.

I wanted to wipe away the tears that flowed from the eyes of the woman with the nose ring when she said, *"My husband took our four children and divorced me. I was forced to return to my father's home. My brother sold me to this man."* My left hand went impulsively to the woman's cheek. I regained my wits when she saw my long nails. I quickly pulled my hand back. Though it was a bit odd, this tender motion of mine put a smile on the face of the woman with the nose ring. Then I listened to the other women's stories, one by one. The smutty woman told what had befallen her, saying, *"My husband brought me here. He said, **'We're divorced!'** in front of the door, stuck the money in his pocket and drove off in his car."*

The blue-eyed woman who hadn't uttered a word since the moment I entered the room, said, *"My husband died in battle. I had nobody, no mother, no father, no children. Narmin told me, **'Let's get you married to someone I know, so you don't die of hunger.'** I trusted her this far."* The woman with hennaed hands didn't even speak, she just cried. I didn't want to bother her, for fear of opening her wounds. I only said how nice her teeth were just to cheer her up a bit. But that made the poor woman even sadder. She continued weeping, saying, *"If only they weren't that way."* I didn't understand that moment why she said that and why my complimenting her teeth caused her to cry even more.

We had reached the bottom of the pot when I told about my uncle's dastardly deeds. But I still had more questions to ask. I told about what I heard while I was in the bathroom the day before. I asked, *"This guy wants to have a night of nuptials with me. Does he want to make everyone his wife like me?"* I got pissed off when the smutty woman said, *"It means he likes you."* I raised my voice somewhat to say, *"Who cares if the old fuck likes me? His liking me only wants me to throw up."* The woman with the nose ring smacked my knee, brought her pointer finger to her mouth, motioning me to shut up. The smutty woman was sad with my outburst. She put the lump of rice in her hand back in the pot and looked into my eyes. In a hushed voice, she said things that both burned my heart and made it skip a beat or two in a tender tone, as though she was talking with her daughter.

She said the armed man didn't bring her here to become his wife, but rather to sell her to someone else coming from other cities, or even from Lebanon or Turkey. I felt she was going to faint while telling me how two women were sold in front of a man just a few days ago. I imagined myself in that state when she said they were lined up in front of a man in his seventies who, from his outfit and stance, was clearly quite wealthy. I thought I would've spat in the face of that old man who picked women like he was buying some chocolate from a market shelf. For someone who checked the whiteness and soundness of the teeth and checked out the legs and breasts of women lined up in front of him, I was sure that at the very least he deserved to be spat on. However, when the smutty woman utter the minute detail, *"Waheed was waiting at his side with his gun on his back,"* I was sure I was going to die in Shroud Lady's house and buried without a shroud while realizing my death wish.

"Girl, look, I don't even know your name, but you're the youngest of all us in this room. I'd want you to suffer the least agony. As he wanted to sleep with you, he is not going to sell you. Allah knows, but rather than becoming the wife of a heartless man in some place you have no idea about, it might be better for you to stay in this house." After hearing these words, I hugged the neck of the smutty woman tightly and I begged her for forgiveness. Then I picked up the lump of rice she left in the pot and made her eat. We all grinned. But our grins were short-lived as the door swung open and Shroud Lady Narmin pounced on us, yelling, *"I've had enough of your nagging, hurry up, get in line for the bathroom, I got other things to do, I can't deal with your shit."*

We got in line to go to the bathroom from prison cell-like doors that were opened and locked. Those who finished their business would return to the room while another one would go into the bathroom under the surveillance of the Shroud Lady Narmin. I was the last one to come out of the room. When I entered the bathroom, I waited for Shroud Lady Narmin to lock the door behind me. I opened my left hand which I had held in a fist for hours and flexed my palm so I could relax my fingers. I looked at my nails and prayed they would grow a bit longer until my period ended, and even before it finished. Then I tossed my dirty headscarf into the trash bin that I'd been hiding in my bosom. Afterwards, I removed the white rag I had stuffed into my underwear and checked it. Even though it was bloody, I didn't throw it away. I would be unable to find another rag to use. I repositioned it in my underwear after folding it so the blood stains were inside and the clean side faced upward. I spoke with a piece of shroud while doing this, saying, *"Right now you can only reach this part of my body, shroud, but you're not going to wrap my entire body, because whatever happens, I'm not going to die!"*

I stayed in that room which was nothing more than a prison cell for another four days. It held four women at the foot of four walls with me sitting right next to the door. We had trouble breathing in this unventilated, hot room. We only came together once a day while eating our meal. We were eating the same old uncooked rice prepared at the same temperature from the same tray with our hands. We got our problems off our chest while we ate. But the moment we consoled each other, Shroud Lady Narmin would come charging in. We would come and go to the bathroom with the same routine. I didn't return to the same place when I emerged from the bathroom in the evening of the fourth day.

Shroud Lady Narmin asked me whether my period had ended before she locked me in the bathroom. When I said it was still going on, she said, *"That's enough of your lying. Throw away the headscarf you got between your legs and wash your pussy,"* as she locked the door behind her. I was shocked. But I quickly pulled myself together. I was going to experience this situation sooner or later. I opened my left fist and gazed at my nails. They still weren't very long, but I was sure they were going to do me some good by giving me strength. I wasn't even praying, *"I hope I won't be needing these."* Because I knew damn well I was going to need those nails. I only prayed for both the opportunity as well as the strength in order to use my nails. For this I moved my left hand for a while, relaxing my fingers. Then I removed the rag I shoved into my underwear. I found a tiny spot in the inner part of the rag that wasn't blood smeared. I positioned the shroud piece in my underwear and didn't do anything as Shroud Lady Narmin had commanded. I pounded on the bathroom door saying, *"My Allah, give me the force."*

Opening the bathroom door, Shroud Lady Narmin looked at my face with a weird expression. I couldn't tell whether she pitied me or was jealous of me. But unlike previous days, her face bore no anger. As I walked in the corridor behind Shroud Lady Narmin, I stopped involuntarily in front of the room where the other women were kept. My legs trembled fearfully. Not even a speck remained of the courage that enveloped my body in the bathroom a few minutes ago. I looked pleadingly at Shroud Lady Narmin, who understood I had stopped and turned around. My eyes said, *"Lock me up in this room again."*

It was no longer my dream to go back home and reunite with my mother. I wanted to be able to return to the room where I was held with the four women. The grim, furious state of Shroud Lady Narmin was back in a flash. *"Don't waste time there, you little whore, your place is here tonight,"* she said as she showed me the door of the side room. It was all so clear that jealousy lurked below this angry sentence. At that moment, I wanted to shout out, *"Was it me who arranged your husband, bitch, you were the one who imprisoned me here."* I was afraid of being on the short end of slim Shroud Lady Narmin's fury before entering a room where I didn't know what would happen to me. If she wanted, she could've meted enough harm to keep me from staying on my feet. That's why I kept silent, leaned my head forward in submission as I entered through the door she opened.

I was looking at the mattress on the floor while the door was being locked behind me. As it was, there was nothing else in the room besides a Quran hanging on the wall. The sheets and pillowcases were made from Narmin's shroud cloth. Getting into that bed meant death for me, and those pillowcases were going to be my shroud. Just as a challenged the shroud piece I positioned in my underwear in the bathroom, I called out to pillowcases in the same manner: *"You're not going to wrap my body, I'm not getting into that bed, and come hell or high water, I'm not going to die!"*

When Waheed entered the room, I went into the opposite corner of the room to put some distance between us. I began waiting on my feet and was no longer making a fist with my left hand, just flexing my palm to relax my fingers. But my plan was to try to first to see if Waheed had a heart or not. I wasn't very hopeful, but it was worth a try. If there wasn't a grain of humanity left in him, I was going to use my nails to get the hell out of there. I had no further plans. My nails had to come through for me. While mulling over my situation, I was trying to stay strong, but my legs were trembling again. I was forcing myself not to collapse in a heap on the floor. I leaned my back onto the wall, closed my eyes and took a deep breath. I had to stay alert so I wouldn't die. My eyelids were like a television screen. I was watching my mother, my father and my brother. We were smiling and embracing at each other with yearning. I panicked and opened my eyes with the sound of the keys.

The sweet dream behind my eyelids ended abruptly with Waheed's ugly appearance. He was standing there facing me with his gun on his back. He was wearing a white tah-wb which was the same material as Shroud Lady Narmin's. It was as if everything that day had turned into a shroud and was telling me I was going to die. But come hell or high water, I wasn't going to die. Waheed gave me a dirty grin, then turned around and shut the door. He removed his weapon and laid it down slowly on the edge of the bed. I began pleading the moment he removed his tah-wb. I didn't want to cry, but tears were flooding down my cheeks. I was saying, *"Uncle, please don't touch me. I'm still a little girl, for Allah's sake, don't do anything bad to me."* I also called him grandpa a couple of times so that maybe he'd think about the age difference between us and be ashamed. But he didn't give a shit. The more I cried, the more apparent the dirty grin appeared on his face.

He was only wearing a sirwal -a long white pant which is worn underneath-. I saw scars on his arm and chest that he most probably got in battle. I revolted, *"My Allah, good people get killed by dropping flowerpots on their heads, so why didn't you take the life of this crook who has this many scars on him?"* As he moved towards me, he rubbed his bearded with one hand, and rubbed between his legs with his other hand. I got sick to my stomach when I saw his swollen dick between his legs. I was on the verge of throwing up. He was two steps away when I leapt from my place like a rabbit so he wouldn't get next to me. I ran into the other corner of the room taking pains not to step on the bed.

Waheed's filthy grin was replaced by a disgusting frown. He shouted, *"What, are we going to play* **'puss-in-the-corner'** *until the morning, get your butt in the bed."* Meanwhile, he removed his sirwal. I could no longer bear the scene across from me as I cramped up forward and vomited. Vomit spewed across practically half the bed. My face and arms were covered in barf. I could see the uncooked rice grains on top of the white bedsheet. I actually didn't plan to throw up on the bed. I was hoping that Waheed would be impacted by this scene and maybe change his mind. He didn't stop, was so blinded by anger to the extend of wanting to rape me on top of the vomit. One of his hands was still busy rubbing his penis. It was clear he had shaved around his penis and just as it's sinful not to shave the groin area, it's also fine for these bastards to rape girls with the same dick.

I needed to make one more move that moment to implement my final plan. I sprung from where I was two steps before he reached him. This time, I was in the other corner of the room. Sticking my hand under my skirt, I removed the piece of shroud from my underwear in an instant, throwing it in Waheed's face as he sauntered over to me, swearing under his breath. I shouted, "I'm on the rag, you infidel sonofabitch." He kicked away the bloody rag that fell to the floor. There was nothing else for me to do in the face of this naked monster. He was turning gigantic with every step he took. I was going to either take out his eye else I was going to scare him out of his wits. I quickly removed my underwear. Thinking I was going to submit to him, he put back on his filthy grin. He slowed his movements down. I leaned against the wall to pull myself together. Figuring I wouldn't be able to use my nails while on my feet, I slid down the wall to sit on the floor.

My skirt was at my waist and my legs were spread out. Like a rabid dog frothing at the mouth, Waheed glued his eyes between my legs as I lifted my left hand into the air, shouting, "You want this, you animal, do you want this?" Waheed looked at my left hand and didn't comprehend what I said. After I yelled again, *"I'll die first before I submit to you, you Allahdamn bastard!"* I quickly dropped my left hand into my pubes.

My left hand was in my pubic area for perhaps a minute or a few minutes. I was on the verge of passing out from all the pain. But I knew I was near my end. There was no other way out of there. Maybe I was committing suicide. But even at that moment, I didn't want to die without giving it a fight. I locked my eyes on Waheed. He still had a stunned look on his face. I retracted my left hand from my groin and lifted it into the air in a fist. Blood that leaked from my palm was dripping down my arm. There were pieces of flesh between my nails. I couldn't bear to look at my groin for fear of fainting. I could see Waheed's groin. The last scene I saw was the deflation of the thing Waheed wanted to stick between my legs, then I blacked out.

When I woke up, I found myself at the foot of a wall again. I regained my wits somehow and sat with my back up against the wall. I was faced by a desert ridge and surrounded by piles of rubbish. A revolting stench burned my nose. I looked at my grimy hands and saw dried blood stains on my left hand. I looked for what seemed to be an eternity at my nails that got me out of that rape chamber. There were still scraps of flesh between them. I couldn't get up the courage to check my groin area for fear it would be too agonizing. I gazed out at the opposite ridge then looked at the wall behind me. It was the same as the garden wall of Waheed's house and I figured I was in the backyard of the house. I pondered why Waheed tossed me out here. Maybe he thought I was dead, or maybe he left me here to die. But in the end, I didn't die, not by a long shot.

I didn't want to sit beneath the burning sun much longer. I hurried, afraid that either Waheed or Shroud Lady

Narmin would come out to check on me. I got to my feet, clinging to the wall. I started off taking slow steps. As I turned at the foot of the wall, I saw the dirt road my uncle had brought me here. I walked silently from the foot of the wall. Extending my head slightly from the corner, I checked to see if the garden door was open or not. Nobody was in sight, so I began walking quickly towards the direction I came with my uncle.

I intended to make a sprint for it, but I couldn't manage. My feet were naked and the stones were painful. But my real pain was coming from my groin area. The more I tried to make quick movements, the more I was like screaming in pain. Then again, I was doing the best I could to walk quickly. I never turned around to see if anyone was coming. As I proceeded, I was muttering, *"C'mon, Waheed, if you see me, just draw your weapon and shoot me."* That's because I didn't have the strength to put up the same struggle again. I was lucky that neither Waheed nor Shroud Lady Narmin saw me. Maybe they saw me and just didn't want to bother with me anymore, I don't know.

I began to notice homes and cars at the end of the dirt road. I was a total wreck; my left hand and skirt were bloody. I was barefoot and everyone was looking at me curiously. If I say my address, maybe someone would help me find my way. But I was so scared out of my mind that I didn't want help from anyone. Of course, I didn't know where I was. My goal was to walk just to the end of the avenue. Then I didn't know where I was going to gIo. An elderly lady coming out of a bread bakery came over next to me. I was startled, thinking I was caught by Shroud Lady Narmin. I looked at her face in fright when she said, *"Girl, what's happened to you? Don't you have a house to go home to?"* She was another woman and was looking at me with concern. She was persistent, continuing to ask me what had happened to me and where I was going. I began to cry. My energy was totally depleted. I collapsed on top of the woman. I vaguely remember her shouting out, *"Ahram, get in here quickly."* A man came running out of the bakery. Later on, I learned these nice people who carried me inside were husband and wife. They had me drink some water, then they washed my face. They brought me some food, but I didn't feel like eating anything. They insisted that I eat a few bites of bread. Thanks Allah, I had been rescued and was in the hands of some decent people.

After pulling myself together somewhat in the bakery, I told them who I was and where my home was. Although they insisted quite adamantly, I didn't tell them my troubles. I could only respond by saying, *"For the love of Allah, please take me home."* Finally, they backed down from asking me questions. I was breathless from all the excitement when they said, *"C'mon we're taking you home."* I thought of father again. He died in a bakery and I found life in another bakery. Ahram, whom I later learned was the owner of the bakery, had me sit in the trailer hooked to the back of his motorbike.

It hurt too much for me to sit straight up in the trailer. I leaned against his wife, who sat next to me. She embraced me, as I flashbacked to the ruthless arms of shroud seller Narmin I was in just yesterday. That moment, I was in the arms of a compassionate woman whose name I didn't even know. I cried the entire way for the shit I went through as well as for this paradox. Dust kicked up by the wind mixed with my tears, sticking to my cheeks. I couldn't stay put from the excitement I felt when we pulled into the street where our house was. I tried to get out of the trailer even before the motorbike came to a full stop. I was so weak, I crumpled to the ground. But I didn't care about the pain I was in. I straightened up where I fell and sat up sidewise. My face froze on our home. I was crying but I was happy as I was reuniting with my home and my mother.

The shriek of my mother, who opened the door after hearing the sound of the motorcycle, is still ringing in my ears. She came out running in her barefeet over to my side. She landed on top of me where I sat. We cried for what seemed hours in the middle of the street. I leaned my back against the spot I trusted the most, my mother. My hands were in my mother's hands. She put her cheek on my cheek, asking, *"I looked everywhere for you. Where were you, my girl, where's your uncle?"* I turned my head behind me, and she was overcome with fear when I said, *"Didn't the bastard come back?"* Mother said my uncle Ubeyd didn't come back and his wife and four kids haven't been seen either, since we left together to find my brother. Mother went silent when I asked, *"What about my brother?"* I went silent as well.

From: Yusuf
Subject: **Helplessness is such a shitty situation**
September 23rd, 2014

I **tried persuading Hifza to go** see a doctor for almost a whole week. She objected the more I said, *"Let's go together and not delay this treatment any longer."* She was embarrassed and didn't want people to know the reason for her doctor visitation. When in fact, she had nothing to be embarrassed about as she was a heroine. I was amazed about the struggle she fought in confronting death, rape and lowlife scumbags. I was also astounded by her tenacity to survive. I also felt the pain of her wounds that were opened in her fragile body and sensitive soul inside me.

The night she told me of the hell she went through, I suppressed my hiccups as I cried so nobody would hear my voice. I murmured to myself, *"Life's not fair"* as I wiped my tears on my pillow. Ultimately, life was testing all of us with preferences that weren't fair at all. Some were being tested with death or suffering that was worse than death, while others were being tested with the problem whether their fat asses would fit in skinny trousers. The deep wounds or light scratches that these tests left on us were called fate. I couldn't just say, *"Hey, that's Hifza's fate"* and accept all this much cruelty. I knew there was nothing I could possibly do for those who remained behind. I swore to have her forget the pain of her past. From now on, I was going to be at Hifza's side, regardless of whatever tests she's faced with. I was in love with her and it was my duty to find the salve for her wounds.

My persuasive efforts that lasted nearly a week finally paid off when Hifza conceded to visit the doctor under the condition it be kept strictly between us. We went out saying we were going to wander about Taksim and visited an obstetrician. She was a woman doctor and her private clinic was located on the same avenue as the pickle shop. It was important for the doctor to be a woman to curtail Hifza's embarrassment. We were lucky the doctor really knew her job well. She was like a sweet kindergarten teacher who managed to get a shy kid to smile and get her up to play cheerful games. She took a close interest in Hifza. Hifza's face was beaming when she emerged from the examination room after nearly half an hour. When she stuck a prescription in my hand, I asked her how much we owed her. She said, *"You don't owe me anything. All you need to do is buy the medication."* I was stunned. In fact, I had even borrowed some money from my mother, telling her I was going to buy a pair of shoes. After all, Hifza had no insurance coverage and moreover, we were at a private clinic. I insisted on paying, but the woman doctor looked in my face and smiled, *"Life doesn't always open wounds, there are some tricks to dressing those wounds."* She asked us to return the following week for a checkup as she went back into her examination room to treat her next patient.

I asked Hifza what happened in the examination room, the doctor didn't take any money. I was further surprised when Hifza said, *"The doctor was going to call the police!"* She must've suspected such a situation. Even children knew that cases of child brides had increased after the arrival of the Syrians. In fact, kids were most familiar with the situation. When the doctor persisted, *"Who did this to you? Come on out and just tell me,"* Hifza was afraid I would get in trouble so told the doctor everything that had happened to her. Thus, I understood why she was stuck in the examination room for so long. Because I was scared the reason the examination lasted so long was that her wound was malignant. Hifza said there was nothing to be afraid of. *"My wounds would heal quickly if I applied the salve and antibiotics regularly that the doctor wrote up. A plastic surgery won't even be necessary,"* she said shyly. I didn't ask her anything else for fear of embarrassing her even more. But she looked like could've said more had I pressed her.

I wanted her to say what was on her mind. *"Hifza, tell me whatever the doctor said, don't be embarrassed for Allah's sake!"* I laughed involuntarily when she bent her head to the floor and said hoarsely, *"She also told me I needed to sit in a tub of warm water for about fifteen minutes a day until I got better."* I said, *"Is that why you're embarrassed, sweetheart? Hey, I've got a washbowl in the bathroom where I let my white shirts soak in hot water. You can use that. Nobody would understand."* I hugged her and kissed her on the cheek. When she put her head on my shoulder, I could feel how much she trusted me and that she loved me a lot. We picked up the prescribed antibiotics and salve from the pharmacy, then I left Hifza at home. She brightened my life once more when she thanked me with her cute accent before entering the flat.

As I had to take Hifza to the doctor, I went to the pickle shop in the afternoon. My life was ruined again when I saw *dangalak* Hayri's face, who gave me time off with the excuse that I was going to do some shopping with my mother. Hayri had turned into even more of a picklepuss ever since his mother Fatma had arrived from the country. In order not to put up with his surly attitude, I went into the back part of the shop with the excuse of bringing up goods from storage. I was in the middle of the pickle jars in the storage room and selecting some of them to take to the front side in order to fill in the missing ones on the shelves.

I didn't need to pick so many jars. That's because business had come to a screeching halt after dangalak's fight with horse-head Mahmut. Not only were pickle sales off, but so were those of the honey and molasses that aunt Fatma had brought from the country. When in fact, the five grates of honey she brought this time last year were sold out in a few days. This time around, we were able to sell perhaps only two jars of them per week. Aunt Fatma was shocked and pissed off at the same time. She had been arguing with her son since the day she arrived. She was saying that business was bad due to Hayri's incompetence. She kept saying, *"What a stupid son I've got. Instead of running his business with ordinary Muslims, he's got himself all mixed up with the Islamists like it was a big deal."* They were arguing again when I came out into the front side with jars in my chest. Aunt Fatma got off her stool the moment she saw me and started taking the jars I was carrying and placing them on the shelves. Meanwhile, she continued bitching at her son.

I was getting a kick out of Hayri getting bitched at by

his mother. I could guess that Hayri hated his mother for bitching at him in front of me. Hayri could no longer take it and blew up at his mother as she was placing the last jar on the shelf, shouting at her, *"What do you know about trade, woman? Go and sit at home."* Aunt Fatma lifted up the jar she was about to place on the shelf. I sensed her intent and made an immediate grab for the jar. After Hayri's fight with horse-head Mahmut, I didn't want to clean up pickles and chunks of glass scattered all over the floor again. I took the pickle jar from her and placed it on the shelf, saying, *"Aunt Fatma, it'll be a shame, don't throw it!"* Aunt Fatma used this action of mine as a weapon against her son. She chastised Hayri even more, saying, *"How about that, even this kid is smarter than you. He'd look after the shop better than you if I handed it over to him instead."* Hayri went ballistic, flying to his feet with such force that his leather chair smacked the wall behind him.

The weapons drawn in this fight were clearly apparent. Aunt Fatma was accusing Hayri of incompetence and being stupid enough to change his social circle despite being a local merchant. She was firing straight at Hayri's heart, with the words, *"How about that, not even one of your old customers drops by the shop anymore!"* Hayri was powerful enough to imprison his wife at home but his mother was a woman with claws. She wasn't getting crushed by Hayri's salvos. Just as he did whenever he was in dire straits, Hayri clung to the religious card. His intention was to beat his mother's womanhood over religion and manlihood by saying *"Shut up already, for Allah's sake mother, this is trade, it's a man's business. You're always sticking your nose in things you don't know about."* Nonetheless, aunt Fatma totally trashed this strategy of Hayri's. She said, *"If it's a man's business, why haven't you managed it? Did you forget your manlihood?"* Their argument turned into a combat from this moment on.

_Mother, let's get one thing straight, you're a woman who was created from the rib of a man. Know your place, don't commit sin.

_Who says that?

_It's in the verses, mother, in the verses. You would've known had you read the Quran.

_You don't even know what you read. Look at the Nisa sura, what does Allah say? *"O mankind, fear your Lord, who created you from one soul and created from it its mate and dispersed from both of them many men and women."*

_Knock it off, Mother you think you know more than the scholars! They explain the meaning of the verses.

_ Is a servant going to add meaning to the word of Allah? Doesn't Allah tell his servants himself whenever he wants to get himself across?

_Mother, don't go any further. That women were created from a man's rib. Why are you objecting?

_I didn't fall out of your rib. You came out of between of my legs.

I can't explain the look on Hayri's face. I mean, it was like a punching bag that was exposed to a hundred quick, consecutive jabs. I looked at aunt Fatma, who was still pissed off. She could no longer stay in the shop. She went out, saying, *"I'm going home, I don't give a damn what you do anymore!"* I looked behind her in stunned amazement. It was incredible how she shut her misstra-know-it-all son down with Quranic verses. Only those like Aunt Fatma could remain undaunted by Hayri's shrieks of *"The verse is like that!"* he constantly threw in our faces in order to render the blind fanatics who poison us even more righteous than thou. I made another decision that day. I was going to read the Quran in Turkish and memorize verses that pertain to current day situations. That way, I'd be able to throw the lies of these religious freaks back in their faces. As it was, my not having read the Quran in Turkish until now was an act of sheer idiocy. I found that reading the words of the creator I was faithful to, in Arabic of which I understood nothing and only knew the alphabet to be extremely illogical. It was not my intent to only read interpretations of verses. I decided to read the Quran directly from Turkish. That's because the words of Aunt Fatma, *"Is a servant going to add meaning to the word of Allah?"* are ringing in my ears. She was totally right.

After aunt Fatma left us, I began cleaning up. I also watched Hayri on the sly. He was in such a devastated state of mind, I suddenly felt sorry for him. But I quickly pulled myself together when chicken guy Selami dropped into the shop. I couldn't even show Hayri any compassion just because of his close friendship with that chicken guy Selami. Even if he was the last person on Earth, there was no way Selami could have aroused the feeling of pity in me. I couldn't even look in Selami's face with that hatred. I didn't get the greeting he gave. Of course, he started in again with his mumbling to the tune of, *"Take the greetings of Allah."* I wanted nothing of it. I turned my butt around and continued dusting off the jars.

Normally, Hayri would rip into me for dissing Selami. But this time, he looked like he couldn't give a shit about the situation. His head was stuck out in front, contemplating his navel. Selami's greeting was left suspended in midair. In fact, when Selami said, *"Hey, there's the call to prayer, c'mon, let's head over to the mosque,"* he didn't even lift his head and look into Selami's face. He blew off Selami, mumbling, *"You go ahead, I'll catch up." "Fine, don't be late"* grumbled Selami, sulking on his way out.

I wouldn't be lying if I said I started feeling sorry for Hayri just because he sent Selami packing that way. I despised Selami. My hatred for Selami and all those like him was based on vast experience accumulated. I witnessed how the majority of the senior citizens in our community who appeared cute and chubby on the outside were really hateful and arrogant on the inside. These people whom we showed respect due to their age and whom we never expected any evil were the main source of ignorance and corruption that poisoned our lives. There was a malicious smile on my face while I pondered all this. First Aunt Fatma taught Hayri a big lesson, then Hayri showed Selami the door. Could it possible for me not to be happy after witnessing these two events?

While continuing to dust off the jars with a feather duster, I watched Hayri from the corner of my eye. He was sitting at the table, his hand on his face and his eyes were glued to the table. He was so quiet and motionless that it wasn't even clear if he was breathing or not. He had calmed down considerably after ISIS' pickle ban and then the rock'em sock'em up with horse-head Mahmut. He came to the shop early, and except for idle chat with the few customers who came into the shop to buy pickles, he sat meekly at the table for hours until closing time. He didn't even turn on his computer. Perhaps he was afraid of reading more news about another ban. All in all, it was never clear when and on what matter the ISIS leaders would issue a fatwa. I mean, the mentality that bans the placing of eggplants and tomatoes in the same plastic bag for their sexual connotations, could also issue a fatwa demanding that all pickle shops close completely. Then again, Hayri's stagnation had attained such a degree that he could no longer boss me around. Of course I wasn't complaining about this. But, one thing's for sure, his getting chewed out by his mother sure put him in a serious funk. Because regardless of the funk he was in, the Hayri I knew had such a reckless character, he could spew a ton of bleepable obscenities at his mother whenever he got pissed off.

Fearful that Hayri would realize that I was spying on him, I began looking at the shelves next to him. I pretended to survey the shelves like I was looking for missing goods. While looking for the heck of it, I realized there were no pickled plums on the shelf. I headed towards the storage room swinging my feather duster as I went. Just when I was muttering to myself, *"With Allah's help, you'll complete your evolution and become a person amongst people,"* Hayri suddenly got to his feet. I thought he was going to say something to me, but he didn't say a single word. He sauntered on by me without even looking in my face and exited the shop. As a matter of fact, he didn't don his turban and tabard he had removed in anger while arguing with Aunt Fatma. It was kind of strange, considering he never went to the mosque without his turban and cloak. Of course, I wasn't curious where he went. It was none of my business. It was enough to know he wasn't next to me or near me. Besides, I had other problems to mull over instead of I worried about Hayri. I had Hifza in my life now, Hifza…

My phone rang just as I was going into the storage room. It was my brother Muhsin calling. Allah knows what problem he had, but I couldn't just ignore his call. After all, he had a place in the line of fate leading up to my meeting with Hifza. The day he rang and said, *"Hurry and get home, your mother's waiting!"* was the day I saw Hifza in our flat. I could even put up with my brother Muhsin for this role in my getting acquainted with Hifza. In fact, despite my brother Muhsin being such a complete dangalak all the time, I had a guilty conscience due to the scar I left on his nose. If only the animal hadn't jumped on top of a ten-year old kid and spitting in his mouth as a show of force while fighting over the remote control. At the very least, had he treated me like a person when I was little, I wouldn't have landed my first and only punch on his nose. I mean, the reason that let my conscience gripe was still brother Muhsin's being a dangalak, but the shit he did still didn't require me to break his nose.

I answered the call. *"Hurry up and come home."* he said gruffly. Though I asked, *"What happened again bro, what's up?"* he insisted me to get home asap. He didn't even hang on my question *"Did something happened to Hifza?"* Normally, he would've jumped on my shit, saying, *"Your mother is at home, if you're going to worry about someone, you better start worrying about her first."* He didn't take that route. It was obvious the situation was serious.

I went back from the storage door. I tossed the feather duster in my hand onto Hayri's armchair. I figured at any rate Hayri wouldn't be coming back. He's got another migraine, so I closed the shop at noon. I also couldn't wait for his wife he imprisoned at home to call me either. If only she called me at that moment, the poor woman would have the opportunity to speak hoarsely with someone besides Hayri. If only I could get the wretched woman to speak as long as possible and get her to feel she is alive. There was nothing else I could possibly do other than to offer my prayers once more *"My Allah, please give this woman's voice back to her."*

The hodge-podge of footwear in front of the door was a sign something out of the ordinary was happening inside. Amongst the shoes that were removed hastily, I recognized those of my elder brothers Harun and Yahya. However, there were also the shoes of a man and a woman in front of the door. From the sound of the voices coming from the living room, there was a heated argument going on in the flat. Actually, I had to go to the toilet really bad. But when I heard the noise from inside, I put off going to the toilet and went straight into the living room. My mother and brothers were sitting in the armchairs, while Hifza was sitting in the chair next to the television. Aunt Meryem was standing and all eyes were on her. She was shouting at an old man and woman sitting next to each other on the sofa. From what I gathered she had the old man in her crosshairs. She was yelling, *"You sold me and got the money, you sold my ID and you got the money, what, you haven't got your fill yet, you Allahless infidel!"* She was looking so furiously in the old man's face that she didn't even notice my entrance.

I made eye contact with Hifza. I nodded my head as if to mean, *"What's going on?"* She pouted and lowered her head. I couldn't bear the melancholy on her face. I passed in front of my mother and brothers and went over to Hifza's side. I asked loudly, *"What's going on, Hifza, who are these guests?"* The moment Hifza lifted her head to respond, Aunt Zehra's voice reverberated in the living room. I looked in the old man's face while she shouted, *"This guy is my thug brother, Bahattin, and this is his wife."* The trickster Bahattin who totally screwed up my father's life was sitting right across from me, and he really looked like a total thug. Despite all Aunt Zehra's insults there wasn't a grain of tension or the feeling of shame in the man's face. On the contrary, he looked in Aunt Zehra's face and smiled, saying insistently, *"Sister, calm down and let's talk."* I couldn't bear anymore and intervened. I held Aunt Zehra's hand and took a seat next to my mother, *"Let it be, what is he going to want?"*

While taking a seat, I gawked at aunt Zehra's face when she said, *"He wants your house."* What right could this guy have to want our house! With the same shocked expression, I looked first at my mother, then my brothers. They were at least as surprised as me. They looked dumbfounded and as it was, didn't even say a single word. Somebody had to intervene in the midst of all these stunned faces and that person was me. First, I need to understand what Bahattin really wanted. In fact, I had to first know how he found our home, and how he knew that Hifza and her mother were here. I now had everyone's attention. I took a chair from the dining table and sat next to Hifza. I turned to Bahattin with an angry expression on my face and acquaint myself first. I told him that I was the the youngest son of Abdulkadir, whose life he fucked up with a thousand tricks.

_Before we get into that business of wanting the house, go on and tell us from who did you hear that Aunt Zehra and Hifza were here, and how did you find our address?

_Of course, I heard when they arrived and learned their address. They are my family.

_So, if they are so important to you, why didn't you call them or ask about them for thirty years?

_Our family business doesn't concern you. I came here

to protect my sister. This house and the fields back in the country are my sister's. The widow's pension your mother withdraws is also my sister's. That is, whatever was Abdulkadir's belongs to my sister. I can't allow someone to abuse her right.

_What a bunch of crap! This is our house. Nobody's rights are abused in this house.

_This house is not yours by a long shot. Who is Abdulkadir's official wife? Zehra! That's why everything that Abdulkadir left behind is Zehra's.

I leapt to my feet and clutched Bahattin's throat. I couldn't feel his neck through his long black dyed beard, but from what I could tell when he grabbed my wrists tightly, I hurt him a bit. But he couldn't manage as I side-stepped him. My mother and brothers grabbed me from behind and tried pulling me back. Just then, Bahattin's wife, who had been sitting calmly next to him, decided to jump into the fray. More precisely, she pretended to get involved. We came eye-to-eye and she looked like she was saying, *"Do me a big favor and strangle him."* Commotion ruled the living room when I didn't release Bahattin's throat. Bahattin tried landing another punch, but he missed again. While trying to protect myself, Yahya and Harun managed to free my hands from Bahattin's throat. But the real thrust came from someone I didn't expect. My brother Muhsin gave Bahattin a hard slap upside his head. The atmosphere in living room took on a more omnious tinge to it. The women, including Bahattin's wife were crying while the men were shouting. Bahattin was stuck between me and my brothers as he furtively sought a way out like a rat caught in a mousetrap.

Once again, it was up to my brother Harun, who was a

teacher, to calm us all down. He had my brothers and I sit in the armchairs one by one. He yelled especially at me to shut up, but but I had no intention of shutting up. My brother Harun turned to Bahattin and said, *"Get up and get out, or else the shit's going to hit the fan real quick."* Bahattin threatened with an impudent expression on his face, *"I'm leaving with my sister, and we'll be back. Vacate our house or believe me, that's when the shit's really gonna hit the fan."* I leapt to my feet and was going to go for his throat again had Mother not grabbed my hand. I yelled, *"From whose home are you kicking out whom, you dangalak! Get the fuck outta here, or I'll murder you!"* I was livid because of Bahattin's smug attitude. Just as if it wasn't him who was being strangled a few minutes ago, he still had that bullshit smile on his face. He was so relaxed, he was rubbing his beard with both hands. *"If you don't vacate, I'll have the police and courts evacuate this house by force! You used my sister's ID for years. I'll have you all tossed in prison. I won't let you put one over on my sister."* It was aunt Zehra who wrecked his relaxed demeanor.

_I don't need your help. Don't touch these people, just beat it.

_This house and the monthly salary are yours. Even if you quit going after what's yours, I won't quit. I had Abdulkadir buy that field. He bought this house with the income from that field. But for years he didn't pay the money he promised he would. Now it's payback time.

_I'm not letting this happen.

_Don't raise a stink in vain, Zehra. I'll rat on you to the police and the attorney's office.

_I'll rat on you too. I'll tell them you stole my ID and sold it. I'll tell them how you bribed the census board official.

You're not going to touch as much as a single cent of these people.

_You'll do what I want if you want to see Ahmed.

Bahattin struck Aunt Zehra at her softest spot. A great silence suddenly descended upon the living room. We as a family just gaped at each other. It's quite possible we all had the same question going through our minds that moment. Did Bahattin find Ahmed like he found our house? As he spoke with such self-confidence, he definitely knew something. We wondered what Aunt Zehra was going to do. None of us could figure how Aunt Zehra's would behave when she heard Ahmed's name. Because even if he wasn't found unharmed, at least a light of hope burned at this unexpected moment for Aunt Zehra, who had worn herself sick in order to reach his corpse. The person who burned the light was a dishonest man, but it's not important who lit the light in such a situation. At this conjuncture, Bahattin was able to do whatever he wanted, and we couldn't say a word. After all, she was going to reunite with the child she searched for months.

Aunt Zehra pulled herself together and snapped at Bahattin, saying, "You're lying. You can't know were Ahmed is." But her brother was totally at ease as he described Ahmed, even down to the birthmark on his neck. I was amazed how he obtained all this information. There was no longer any point to this interrogation. Aunt Zehra was begging Bahattin to tell her where her son was. Having not gotten to her feet even during the loudest moment, Hifza also knelt in front of Bahattin, sobbing, *"Where's my brother, please tell us the place."* Bahattin now had the upper psychological edge and had a big smartass smirk on his face. For a long time, he didn't reply to either aunt

Zehra or Hifza.

Mother couldn't bear dragging out this scene for much longer. *"Tell us where the kid is. Don't make these poor people suffer so much. Here, the house is yours and so is the money and whatnot..."* as she handed Bahattin the pension card. Mother came roaring to life when she saw that aunt Zehra was pleading for her son. With a harsh gesture, she took the card back that Bahattin was holding in his hand, shouting, *"You're not getting a single kurus -cent- from this house! I can't let other children suffer so I can get back with my son. If you don't tell me where he's kept, I'll find my son some other way. It's enough to know that he's alive. You've got no idea what I'm going through. I was praying that at least they'd hand me back my son's bones, and now I've learned he's alive. What's more, I'm hearing it from an evil person like you. Allah, who blessed me with this news will no doubt reunite me with my son. So, get out of here now, you infidel!"*

While watching aunt Zehra, I muttered to myself, *"Dear Allah, do you have to force people decent enough not to see their own son so others aren't harmed, to rely on such dishonest men."* We were faced with a battle between good and evil. One party's evil towered as high as mountain peaks while the other's benevolence is as deep as the oceans. It seemed that the evil one was going to emerge victorious through threats and blackmail. However, aunt Zehra was determined not to concede defeat. She was on the verge of making a major sacrifice. My conscience agreed with my mother. She didn't need to make this self-sacrifice. But my mind was on our home. We shouldn't be giving in so easily to this crook, we shouldn't be giving him our house. Meanwhile, I was observing Hifza's heart-breaking state as she cried, kneeling in front of Bahattin. She was tearing herself to pieces in order to see her brother one more time. For a moment I thought how depressed I'd be if my brother Muhsin, whom I didn't love, disappeared like Ahmed. Truly, how did he slap Bahattin like that! When in fact, he was such a light-hearted character that he wouldn't put up a fight or argue if you confiscated his computer, he'd spent his life with.

My brother Muhsin was sitting right next to me, so I looked in his face, which was beet-red, and asked him, *"How did you do that, bro?"* I was dumbfounded when he replied with a sobbing expression that appeared on his face, *"How did I do what?"* When I said, *"Don't you remember, when you smacked Bahattin one?"* *"He was about to hit you, Yusuf. Nobody can touch my brother and I won't let anyone touch him."* I really didn't know he loved me this much. It was the right place for me to cry and rejoice at the same time... I looked at his nose and felt another pang of sorrow. I hit his knee twice with my hand and nodded my head in a show of appreciation. *"Allah damn me for all those bad things I said about you. Let's get through this shit, and I'm gonna give you a big bear hug."*

Meanwhile I looked at Bahattin's wife. More precisely, at the woman whom I thought was Bahattin's wife. I said to her sternly, *"Why aren't you talking? Isn't this guy your husband, why can't you prevent the evil he spreads?"* There was such sadness in the woman's face that I experienced the same regret I had just experienced due to what I had done to my brother Muhsin. If only I hadn't opened my mouth. The wretched woman gestured to her husband with both hands, then opened her arms to the side, as if to say, *"What can I do about him?"* Bahattin smirked, and as if it wasn't his throat I'd tried to strangle a little while ago, said, *"She can't speak. What, you think I'd be crazy to marry a woman who bitches at me all the time?"*

Even if he didn't try to confiscate our house, I'd still beat the shit out of Bahattin for his audacity. I could no longer put up with him. He remained unfazed and insistent although I'd said, *"Aunt Zehra said all she's going to say. It's late, we've heard enough of your shit already. Go on, get up and get out. Otherwise, I'm gonna have to toss you on your butt!"* To the extent of rebuking us for not offering him a glass of water even though he'd been sitting there for how many hours now. *"We're going to take care of this matter today. Don't you know that I've come from the other end of Istanbul? The next time I come, it'll be to move into this house."* Just then, the living room resounded with Aunt Zehra's shrieks. Aunt Zehra rose to her feet again. I thought she was going to lunge at Bahattin's throat. On the contrary, she lifted her hand to her own throat. Continuing to cry at Bahattin's feet, Hifza witnessed this action, got up in fear and hugged her mother. Aunt Zehra hugged Hifza with one hand and stuck the other in her bosom. Fumbling around, she pulled out an immensely long gold necklace dangling from her hand. Looking at Bahattin, she spoke breathlessly.

_Listen here, I don't care what you say, I won't let you touch this house or these people. You're after money, isn't that right? Then take this and leave me and these people alone. You tell us where Ahmed is, too.

_What the heck is that?

_It's a meter gold chain. Don't you remember, my father-in-law gave it to me at my wedding. You looked greedily at this chain that day, too. This chain is yours if you tell us where Ahmed is.

_Give it to me!

I watched how Bahattin eyed the gold chain, thinking how aunt Zehra knew her brother like the back of her hand. He was looking at the chain like a starving jackal salivating over its prey. I sensed that aunt Zehra's non-compromising stance and our reaction had made Bahattin throw in the towel. He wasn't going to be able to buy a house, but he was about to have gold worth perhaps half a house. Just as aunt Zehra was about to hand Bahattin the chain, I prevented her from doing so. I said that she shouldn't give him the chain without him telling us Ahmed's place and in fact, without us contacting him. Although Bahattin looked confused, he didn't react to me from the glare of the shiny gold in his eyes. The words, *"Ahmed is in Greece"* slipped out of his mouth. At first, aunt Zehra didn't understand and asked where Ahmed was again. Bahattin said that her boy was in a refugee camp in Greece, syllable by syllable.

We'd all forgotten the ruthless heated argument we'd been having for around five hours and were wondering how Ahmed had gotten to Greece. That's because none of us believed this claim of Bahattin's. Hifza rebuked him, *"You're lying, what would my brother be doing in that country?"* Aunt Zehra didn't believe her son was in neighbor country either. "Allah damn you, you damned liar!" she said as she began to cry. It was clear she was disappointed. However, I thought it wasn't possible Bahattin would say something to endanger this chain. Maybe Hifza's brother was really in Greece. Bahattin had to prove this by putting us in contact with him if he wanted to take the chain. For this reason, I said to him that if he wasn't lying, then he had to let us speak with Ahmed. However, I said in a stressed tone of voice that he could have the chain if he did this. His eyes were still on the shining gold in aunt Zehra's hand. He said, *"I have a telephone number. I'll give it to you and you make the call. The number belongs to an Afghani who stays in the camp. Say you want to talk with Ahmed and he'll have you speak with him. Plus you can have a video chat…"* He removed his telephone from his pocket and showed a number he registered as his nephew. I registered the number which began with *thirty* into my own phone.

I prevented aunt Zehra while she was on the verge of handing her gold to her brother, saying, *"What are you doing, aunt Zehra, wait a sec, we haven't reached Ahmed yet."* Bahattin blew his top this time, asking, *"What kind of guy are you anyway, I gave you the number, why don't you trust me?"* I said, *"If you were a man to be trusted, you wouldn't be coveting a chain to tell the mother the location of your missing nephew. If you were a man, you'd take this woman by the hand and take her to her son with your own hands.* "He got really pissed off, but he didn't prolong the situation. I was sure he didn't want to rock the boat too far in order not to put the chain in jeopardy.

I registered the number into my phone. Like me, the Afghan refugee had an Iphone. I understood from the Facetime app that showed up on my phone registry. Any other time, I would've debated how a refugee could own an Iphone worth thousands of Turkish liras, but I could only appreciate this refugee for being an Iphone owner as we were able to have a video chat with Ahmed. Providing the refugee was paying for internet services in Greece… I sat next to Aae also curious as they passed behind the armchair and started looking at the phone. I made a Facetime call. It rang for a long time but nobody picked up at the other end. I called again. Then once more. Nobody was answering. I looked at Bahattin and said, *"It's either Ahmed or you can forget about the chain. If it turns out you lied to the point of letting down this woman and this girl, then I'm going to make your life very unpleasant for you."* Bahattin leaned back and calmly said for me to continue calling. He added that he was willing to sit where he was until the Afghan refugee answered his phone. He was also cunning enough to ask for something to eat. He was so shameless to the extent he'd drive even the world's most cold-blooded person up the wall.

Seeing as there was no response to my Facetime calls, I said let's send a regular text. I assumed that the Afghan refugee would come back if he read the text. But what language should we send it in? I couldn't figure if it should be in Turkish or Arabic. I didn't even know what language they spoke in Afghanistan. My brother Muhsin said it would be good to write in Turkish, English and Arabic. Even if the Afghan refugee didn't understand the message, he'll show it to someone else in the camp to translate it for him.

We started writing our message thinking there'd most likely be someone in the camp who'd know one of these three languages. I wrote in Turkish that we were looking for Ahmed, and that his mother and sister were with me. This I converted the keyboard into Arabic and handed the phone to Hifza, who wrote the same message in Arabic. I looked at my brothers when it was time for English. Harun and Yahya were looking at me with frozen looks. My brother Muhsin said, "Give it to me" as he took the phone from my hand. He converted the keyboard back into Latin letters and wrote the message in English. I said to myself,

"No way." I was going to beat myself silly if I witnessed another event that alters my opinion about my brother Muhsin.

We began waiting after sending off three texts one after another. Evening had passed and it was getting towards midnight. I was about to die of starvation. I said, *"Let's eat something."* Actually, nobody, with the exception of Bahattin, felt like eating anything. Bahattin was the only one who looked at me when they heard the word *eat.* Mother got up from his place when saying, *"The food's ready, let me heat it up."* Aunt Zehra and Hifza also followed Mother into the kitchen. I looked at Bahattin's wife and I felt sorry for her. I said, *"Why don't you go into the kitchen as well. The kitchen's through the door on the immediate right."* She nodded her head with a light smile, as if she were expecting this offer. She got up and walked towards the kitchen. Then there were five guys still in the living room. I switched on the television to keep away the bad vibes. I left it on a news channel that came on. I didn't care what the program was broadcasting. It was enough there was noise in the living room and that everyone's eyes were glued to the television set. It was as if all of us were waiting our turns in the lobby of a doctor's office and reading to the final word on the back page of a newspaper that we wouldn't normally pick up.

The tranquility in the living room didn't last long. I was stupid enough to think we were going to remain far from the tension while watching a news station in a country like Turkey. The subject of the discussion program featured on the news channel was about ISIS attacking the Kurdish city of Kobane. One of the speakers was griping how members of ISIS were coming and going from Turkey as they wished while there were 150,000 Kurds who fled the massacre only to be kept waiting at the border. My brother Harun started talking as though he was one of the studio commentators. *"Man, didn't this country's prime minister recently vindicate ISIS, saying, '****It emerged as a consequence of fury confronting governmental pressure?'**** Are you stupid enough to expect a step to be taken by these guys against ISIS?"* as he chewed out the speaker behind the screen.

With an odd defensive reflex, the impudent Bahattin turned to my brother Harun and snapped, *"What did these leaders do other than defend the motherland? May Allah keep them at our side."* After these words, we stopped watching the TV screen and switched to a live, heated discussion between Bahattin and my brother Harun. My brother Harun lined up events the government covered up, from the semi rigs loaded with weapons caught en route to Syria to bribe money filled in shoeboxes. In fact, he couldn't hold back his tears while telling how the company that couldn't ensure proper working conditions was given a wide berth after the disaster at Soma caused the deaths of 301 miners. My curses accompanied my brother Harun's tears as he added how the government leader normalized the disaster by saying, *"That's fate for you,"* how one of the leader's men kicked a miner who fell to the ground on camera, then he obtained a doctor's report, saying he had hurt his foot, not to mention how the Labor Minister got his shirt soiled in the mine.

A single typed of answer came out of Bahattin's mouth for each example my brother Harun gave that highlighted corruption, lawlessness or unscrupulousness. According to him, pious men were running the state and each of the negativities that could take until the morning to tell about were a game of the West which wanted to stop Turkey. Those like Brother Harun were mere instruments in this game. My brother Harun got exasperated at Bahattin's words. He slammed his hand onto the tray stand in front of him and shouted, *"I'd be really upset if you didn't support these politicians. With your ignorance and immorality, you're a desperate case and you're where you should be."* The discussion was not headed for an amicable conclusion at all. First, I shut off the television, which was the reason for the argument. Then, I told my brother Harun he needed to calm down. Looking in Bahattin's face, I said, *"We have to put up with this guy, bro. Forgetaboutit."* Bahattin was so shameless, that he asked, *"Is the food in the kitchen ready yet?"* I was now sure that Bahattin's character was impossible to intervene with. Our salvation rested in the hands of the Afghan refugee we were waiting to hear back from.

While my brother Muhsin went to his bedroom without saying a word, Harun went outside to have a smoke. Yahya also went into the adjacent room to have a phone conversation. Of course, I'm not the idiot of the house and I wasn't about to endure Bahattin much longer. I got up and went into the kitchen. The moment I passed through the door, I found myself in a new weird situation. My mother, Aunt Zehra and Hifza were sitting at the table and looking at the teeth of Bahattin's wife. I asked bewilderedly, *"What are you doing?"* My mother point to the bread on the table and answered, *"It's a shame, the woman can't even eat any bread, all her teeth have fallen out."*

While I wondered when they had become so cordial with each other, my mother turned to the mute woman and continued talking. The mute woman was replying to my mother with an uneven voice, hand gestures and facial mimics. Mother showed her own teeth, saying, *"Look, I've been using these teeth for fifteen years now, and I haven't felt any pain or leaking even once. Go visit the doctor I suggest, he's a boozer, but he's got a steady hand."* I broke in, saying, *"Mother, how can you recommend her a boozer?"* I was a nervous wreck, impacted by the argument I'd just witnessed in the living room. I was laughing. I looked at Hifza, who was laughing as well. On the contrary, my mother was quite serious. She wanted me to sit at the table.

_My teeth were disintegrated. One night, your father came around with some guy. The two were totally plastered. They met at some nightclub. Anyways, they came in and the man grabbed my mouth. He looked at my teeth, then turned to Abdulkadir and said, *"Bring me her on Monday."* Then he left.

_I guess he does good work when he's sober.

_Lemme tell you, so, he wasn't sober! He'd opened a bottle of raki with Abdulkadir that day, too. He drank on one hand and pulled my teeth with the other. Eight of them, to be exact. He mounted a set of teeth a week later, and I swear it was worth all my suffering. And he didn't take a cent.

When I heard this story of my mother's, I questioned once more whether my father was normal or not. Had he still been alive, I would've gone up to him and said, "You're off your Allahdamned rocker!" My mother was every bit as nuts as my father. She was recommending to another woman a man who imbibed raki while extracting teeth. Although I had no doubt about my mother's good intentions, I thought that perhaps she wanted to punish Bahattin by sending his poor wife to an inebriated dentist. After all, we were put through hellish circumstances ever since August and my thoughts regarding my family in connection to these circumstances had eroded. The father I knew wasn't my father and my mother had stories I'd never heard before in my life. Every time I'd encounter my brothers, they were always sticking another unknown matter in my eyes. I now knew that we were far from being an ordinary family. Who knows, there may be tons of other convoluted circumstances and strange stories surrounding my family's past that I'm not aware of! We might not return to our previous ordinary days if we reach Ahmed and shake off the Bahattin scourge currently plaguing us, but at least we'll be rid of the suspense that has entangled us and take a calm, peaceful breath of air. Needless to say, my wish didn't come true that night.

When the Afghan refugee didn't reply to our messages, Bahattin ended up spending the night in our living room. Neither he wanted to go nor did we desire to send him away. While Bahattin was afraid of losing the gold chain, we didn't want to lose the single person who had made contact with Ahmed. While Bahattin snored away in my pyjamas on the sofa in the living room, Hifza, Aunt Zehra, my mother and I were up in the kitchen until the morning light with the phone in the center of the table, anticipating a call or message from Greece. No sound emitted from the phone except a few ad messages. However, I saw how even those few message beeps managed to get aunt Zehra and Hifza all excited. It was a really pathetic scene. I wondered, *"If they get all jumpy over ad messages, how would they react if they saw Ahmed on the screen?"*

I still hadn't found the answer to my curiosity when it got light outside. That's because nobody from Greece had called. Actually, I still harbored my doubts as to whether Bahattin was telling the truth or not. That said, the Whatsapp profile photo of the Afghan refugee was minor evidence that Bahattin wasn't lying. That's because when I registered the number that Bahattin gave me, I checked his Whatsapp profile, which featured a photo of someone middle-aged who looked Afghani. As we became familiar with Afghan refugees before the Syrians, I had an idea about what Afghanis looked like. His name appeared as Ramin. Had Bahattin not found someone who looked like an Afghan wandering about the streets of Istanbul and had his add this information, there was really someone out there named Ramin. But he didn't go beyond being an imaginary hero until he called us.

Mother and aunt Zehra went out of the kitchen at around 5:30 AM to do their morning prayers. Hifza and I were left by ourselves at the table. I was unable to ask her how she was for the past two days. I checked the kitchen door and held her hand, asking her, *"How are you doing?"* She said the medicine had reduced her pain. Smiling, she added, *"Soaking in the warm water is working wonders, too. I'm improving, thank Allah. I can also sit up straight, though not as much as before."* While saying this, she had such an expression of gratitude that I couldn't resist hugging her. I planted a little kiss on her check and whispered into her ear, *"The pain will all end soon, we only need to be patient a little longer."*

I closed my eyes and enjoyed Hifza's exquisite scent that wafted into my nostrils from her neck. That is, until Bahattin popped into the kitchen out of nowhere. As if he was in his house, the thirsty dangalak drove me up the wall when he dove into the kitchen without asking whether if it was okay to come in. I blew up at Bahattin again when he saw the embarrassment on Hifza's face. I filled a glass of water from the faucet and handed it to him. He sipped on the water nice and slow as if he wanted to trash my time alone with Hifza. That moment, I wanted to shove the glass in his hand down his throat like a funnel. I made all sorts of contorted facial expressions so he'd get my drift and get the heck out of Dodge, to no avail. This guy was shameless the moment he woke up. Once he finally finished his water, he went back without even saying thanks. He returned before I could even say, *"Jack Flash sat on a candlestick."* He asked for the direction of Mecca. After the brief span of time we had spent together, had someone asked me, *"How would you describe Bahattin?"* I'd say, *"He's a lunatic who believes he'd be forgiven for all the shit he's caused and that all hearts he broke would be repaired between prayer hours."* I described the direction to Mecca, then he insisted, *"Let's go and pray with the congregation."* I told him to go and pray by himself. He insisted. *"C'mon, let's pray together. If you pray with the congregation, you'll be granted 27-fold good deeds."*

_You're a snake in the grass. You think you can cancel out the sins you committed with worshipping that gives you multiple good deeds, don't you? If you ask me, don't trust that account very much.

I didn't want to give Bahattin such a hard time. We might not be able to find him if he committed some insane shit and took off. Even though we had the number of the Afghan refugee, it was best that Bahattin stay with us as we couldn't imagine what other crap he might pull. That's why I didn't bother Bahattin at the breakfast table. Even if I bothered him, it looked like he didn't care much for me. Having eaten dinner with a voracious appetite the night before, Bahattin was demonstrating the same performance at the breakfast table. He was pissing me off the way he slurped his tea and smacked his lips while eating.

At any rate, I was trying to block Bahattin's strange noises out while talking with the others at the table. As a matter of fact, I even chatted with Bahattin's mute wife. With my mother's help, I was able to understand, though not exactly, what the woman meant to say. I started to take a liking to this woman. I mean, had it not been for that damned Bahattin sitting next to her, I would've said to her, *"Don't go, you can stay here."*

My phone rang during breakfast. Everyone suddenly went silent and looked at my phone in front of me. Even Bahattin's disgusting noises weren't heard anymore as he also eyed my phone inquisitively. Nonetheless, we all got excited for naught as Hayri's name was on the screen. He was probably going to snap at me for not opening the shop early. I didn't answer his call as I couldn't put up with Hayri's bitching in the morning. Instead, I sent him an SMS, *"Hey, we've got guests at home, I have to deal with them. I can't make it in today."* Hayri's reply was rather surprising, "Okay." Normally, he would've done his best to fuck up my entire day, even via an SMS. Looks like Hayri was really bummed out about something. I mumbled to myself, *"If Hayri's mood can change, then there's nothing in this world that can't change."* Everyone gave me a curious look when I lifted my head from the telephone. When I said, *"That was my boss, Hayri who called because I didn't go to work,"* I witnessed the disappointment on Aunt Zehra and Hifza's faces once again. These two guys have been through the same wringer for the past couple of days. I swore under my breath, *"Ramin, you better call. Fuck your phone."*

As luck would have it, Ramin didn't hear my obscenities,

as he hadn't called by the evening. Except Bahattin, his wife and my brother Muhsin, all of us were about to crash for lack of sleep. The possibility of going another sleepless night was made worse because we'd have to do it with Bahattin. The guy kept asking for stuff non-stop. Bring me some tea, turn to channel such-and-such, make me this food… It was like he was staying at a five-star hotel. Plus, the crook was going to take the gold chain as well. There was no way I was going to be holed up with this guy for another night.

I had called Ramin on occasion during the say, thinking he'd answer. I said I'd try it again before sitting down for dinner. I called Ramin from Facetime's video option. The telephone opened even before the first ringing sound ended. The coal black hair, and thin nosed Ramin I saw on his Whatsapp profile was live and facing me. I didn't even have time to think, *"Dude, if you were going to answer so fast, why did you keep us waiting for two days!"* Besides, he wouldn't have understood that if I said it. I shouted, *"Hey, it's Ramin, Ramin's here,"* so loudly, that the entire household, including my brother Muhsin came running into the living room. A bewildered Ramin was speaking in a foreign tongue. He was probably asking who I was. I said, *"We're looking for Ahmed, Ahmed from Syria."*

Ramin wasn't comprehending what I was saying because I was talking in Turkish. When in fact I had thought he'd at least get my drift when I said *Ahmed*. I saw that it wasn't happening, I handed the phone to Bahattin, as I knew they had spoken to each other before. Ramin's tone of voice changed when Bahattin looked into the camera and said, *"Peace be upon you, brother, Ahmed, Ahmed…"* He must've remembered Bahattin. I could tell he was saying positive things from his tone of voice. I turned the screen back to me. Ramin was walking between some prefabricated buildings. As far as I could tell from the illumination in front of the buildings, the surroundings resembled the camps erected for the Syrians in Turkey. With a deft move, Ramin turned from the corner of a prefab building. He was moving so quickly, we could hear his breath from the phone's speakers. He swiftly opened the door of the prefab building and yelled Ahmed's name the moment he entered inside. As I could only see Ramin's face on the screen, I couldn't see how the inside of the prefab looked that moment.

Sitting to my right was aunt Zehra and to my left was Hifza, who was practically laying in my lap so she could see the screen. Both of their heads were preventing me from seeing the screen. Anyways, the inside of the prefab building wasn't all that important. The important thing was that we had finally reached Ahmed. As far as I could tell between the two heads, we were looking at someone who was almost the same age as me with a slightly dark complexion. After hearing aunt Zehra's and Hifza's shrieks of joy, I was sure the young man facing us was Ahmed. I stuck the phone in aunt Zehra's hand and pulled myself away from them. Mother and daughter stuck together just like a magnet. They were crying and talking at the same time, communicating in a little Turkish, but mostly in Arabic.

We were watching aunt Zehra and Hifza like we were watching a movie. We didn't need any subtitles to understand what they were talking about. You know how emotional songs, regardless of what language they're sung in, leave indelible marks in the hearts of their listeners, those sentences of yearning we heard that moment were just like that. My mother was drowning in her tears. Bahattin's mute wife was crying. I saw my brother Muhsin rubbing his eyes with his hand. It was obvious he didn't want anyone to see he was crying. As for me, I was forcing myself not to cry. I knew that if I cried, I wouldn't be able to hold myself back from drowning in sobbing hiccups. That's because there was another load on my back that exacerbated the view facing me. I was carrying Hifza's story to and fro like a burlap sack full of thorns. I thought I'd go to the sink and wash my face, maybe I'd relax a bit, but I was also wondering what Ahmed was saying. In the meantime, I was trying not to miss the sentences that were spoken in Turkish. My power was depleted the moment Aunt Zehra kissed the screen, saying 'my child' and I started weeping. All of us, with the exception of Bahattin, were crying, as we gathered around a common pain. That's because we were all helpless.

You cry if you can't find a cure for persecution on your own, and if the people who need to end the persecution are the oppressors themselves, you end up crying even more. Having no one other than Allah to extend your complain is having no choice other than praying for your loved ones and curse your oppressors. Helplessness is such a shitty situation.

From: Hifza
Subject: **We'll wear out, get injured and, in the end die**
September 30th, 2014

I**was in a village cottage** at the westernmost point of Turkey, in Edirne. I was sitting with my back leaned against the wall in a room that didn't have anything but a sofa bed, a few cushions, a desktop computer on top of a floor tray in the corner and a wall clock with a depleted battery. Greece was just past a field and a river. When in fact, just six months ago, we were a sweet little family who loved each other in our own home in Hasakah and were slumbering away in peace. We never even thought once where Greece was. Our lives were like the squiggly line on a heart attack patient's EKG chart and were flowing so fast and so dangerously. We no longer had any routine and we were living on the edge. We were close to death as we clung to life. We were as close to crying as we were to laughing and being happy. Struggling with our worries in a peaceful moment back then, we were in the same boat in a dim room of this village cottage.

While we were listening to the sound of rain coming down, we wanted it to subside in order to survive. I couldn't watch the rain as I was forbidden to get near the window. I, too, took advantage of the silence of the night and listened to the drops landing onto the ground with a progressively louder noise. Between the falling rain, it seemed I was hearing the things my brother Ahmed told us. It was as if he was standing behind the wall I was leaning my back against, drenched to the bone in the rain, telling what had happened to him in my ear once again. Who knows, maybe my brother also spent his last night in Turkey, in this house…

I thought about my uncle Ubeyd. He was a monster who planned to wipe out the family of his dead brother for his own best interests. After the bombing, he didn't tell us about the shack of a hospital where my brother was recuperating even though he knew. He was so cold-blooded that he went searching for my brother Ahmed with us for days. All the way until he sold me to the ISIS guy. The lowlife picked the day my injured brother got back on his feet to sell me. The day he sold me to the ISIS guy, he went over to my brother and told him without any shame or compunction, *"Your house collapsed in the bombing. I sent your mother and Hifza to Greece. We as a family waited for you to get better. C'mon, we're going to head to Greece too."* But most of all, he burned me when he told my brother, who wanted to see my father's grave before leaving Syria, *"There no cemetery left, he was blown to smithereens."* I knew that while bombs were raining down upon us and bullets were whizzing to and fro, visiting a grave was nothing but choose a tomb for yourself. However, one would want to at least touch the gravestone of someone he'll never see again. We were searching for my brother with that emotion, saying, *"There should at least be a gravestone, where we can go and cry, talk, and get a load off our shoulders."*

There were no words to describe the ruthlessness of my uncle who treated my brother no differently than a beast of burden as they travelled partly by motorbike, partly on foot from Hasakah to Kilis, then on to Istanbul by bus and then on to Edirne by private car that their smugglers had arranged. My hatred for that immoral couple who made my injured brother carry both their huge suitcase and our two-year old cousin would never go away. It's not possible to forgive him for dropping off my poor brother, who hoped to unite with us after crossing the Meric river, in the refugee camp all by himself.

As he took off with his four kids and wife, he said, *"I brought you this far in respect of being the only son of my brother. We're going on to Germany. You'll have to take of yourself from here on in,"* which only evoked the feeling in me to spit in his face. I'll always have the pleasure to spit in uncle Ubeyd's face. That was the place of women in the culture of these honorless guys. You can sell women whenever necessary and build a new life with the money you get. I was absolutely right, of course, it would be a very simple reaction to spit on the face of this bastard who sold me at the expense of me being a *virgin girl*, using that money to hit the road and use my brother as a beast of burden.

While going over the phone conversations in my mind that we had with my brother Ahmed, the host of the home we were staying in came in with a tea tray. Our smugglers who were going to get us into Greece were gracious enough to offer us a pot of tea and this was a very important gesture for me. Being able to drink hot tea in an atmosphere where I couldn't lift my head and look out the window was going to be nothing short of an elixir for me. As our host began to fill the tea glasses, I recalled the last tea I drank from Yusuf's hand at the breakfast table. I wonder what my hero who months later helped me deal with my pain and got me to sit up straight was doing in Istanbul? Was he thinking of me, or was he trying to forget what happened to him over the past two months because of me? My heart would've liked it if he was thinking of me, but my mind, which didn't want to be unfair to Yusuf, wanted him to forget me. I upset Yusuf very much with my coming into his home, with my painful story, with our blazing love, not to mention our headlong departure in the end. The heavy grief that enveloped his face when my mother said, *"We're going to Greece…"* came in front of my eyes when I took my first sip from my tea. He was to first to react to these words of my mother's, when he said, "Where are you going aunt Zehra, can't you have Ahmed come here instead?"

Yusuf also knew that my brother Ahmed wouldn't be able to Turkey the same way he left. He just didn't want to lose me. When I saw the sorrowful shape Yusuf was in, I thought to myself, *"If only my lowlife uncle had left my brother in İstanbul."* Even in his vile state, he might have taken my brother to Greece knowing that Turkey wasn't going to be the best bet for a Syrian. After all, I was following the news every day and understood that Syrian refugees were nothing but a cash cow for the Turkish Government. The more Syrians it accommodated, the more money it received from Western countries. Of course, it didn't matter what conditions they were sheltered in. I was also listening to the commentators telling how Western leaders turned a blind eye to the government for making Turkey another Syria by not sending the Syrians to the

West. After all, as far as Europe was concerned, we Syrians were no different than nuclear waste that shouldn't seep in from the Turkish border. We were the leverage for Turkey to get Europe to accept all its sleazy policies at the same time.

No doubt my mother and I were luckier than the Syrians trying to catch their breathe in the middle of all that sleaze. We were the guests of Aunt Meryem. She was like my second mother. But there were also those like Bahattin. The moment he heard Mother utter the word *Greece*, the opportunist, money grubbing Bahattin gleefully exclaimed, *"Alright, then I'll arrange your smugglers and I'll get a cut, too!"* The glow in his eyes couldn't hide the darkness of his heart as he deftly took the golden chain from my mother's hand. Seeing as he had connections in the smuggling business led us to believe his life was as dark as his heart. It was a damn shame knowing that innocent people like us could get out of their quagmire only through the help of people who have a darkness in their hearts. The world we lived in was truly a brutal place. Luck would have it that salvation from the bad shit created by evil people was found by evil people, who took everything the good people had in return. We had nothing absolutely left after giving Bahattin the gold chain. We couldn't have even dreamt about going to Greece hadn't it been for aunt Meryem.

A week after he exclaimed, *"I'll arrange the smugglers,"* Bahattin came back and said that we'd need to come up with 2,000 Euro per person. Neither my mother nor me had ever seen a Euro in our lives. My mother asked how much that would be in Turkish lira. Bahattin calculated in his head that we'd need about 6,000 TL per person. He also said he wanted 1,000 Euro for himself. But we didn't even have 1,000 TL, let alone 15,000 TL. As this reality sunk in, Mother and I sunk into the armchairs in the living room. As we looked about in desperation, Aunt Meryem interceded. *"Wait a second here!"* as she told Bahattin to take a seat. Then she stepped out of the living room. Like Bahattin, we waited in sullen silence. At one point, Bahatting wanted to drink tea, but I blew him off, as I wasn't in the mood to mess around with any tea at that moment.

As it was, Aunt Meryem appeared in the living room doorway shortly afterwards. Muhsin was standing right behind her. She came in with a stack of money in her hand and sat right next to Bahattin. Then she handed him some of the cash, saying, *"We figured inside that 4,000 Euro made 11,200 TL. So, here's 5,600 TL, that's half the amount. Go give this to your guys. They'll get the rest when they hit the road."* Bahattin gave her a sour look when he heard this, retorting, *"Great, but where's my share?"* aunt Meryem told Bahattin that he'd get his share only whenever we'd reached Greece. Bahattin looked like he was about to cry. Although he insisted on getting his share right then and there, aunt Meryem held her ground. She sent Bahattin packing, saying, *"You know you'll get your money once this woman and this girl arrive safe and sound in Greece, so don't drag on about it! Go and give this money to the smugglers."*

Mother and I were in total shock. Mother was weeping as she said, *"What have you done? As if we haven't caused you enough trouble, you've gone and given him all that money."* Aunt Meryem stuck the remaining amount of money in my mother's hand rather matter-of-factly, then hugged mother's neck. She cried, *"This is nothing compared to the sacrifice you've made. I was saving this money for a rainy day. Looks like that rainy day is today. Go and get back with your son.*" She said that wherever we went in this world, we shouldn't forget we had a home in Istanbul. I had to be stone statue not to shed a tear while they were crying their eyes out. I'd gotten fed up with crying but try telling that to my tears. My life was slipping by in my teardrops. I cried whenever I felt pain and whenever I was totally ecstatic.

My little comrade came over to my side while I was sipping my tea. She gave me a sweet look of a child of five or six years old. Pressing her curly sandy hair that fell to her cheeks behind her ear and caressed her cheek. I couldn't understand how her nose and mouth fit on such a small face. This precocious masterpiece of Allah sat next to me. I asked her her name and she said, *"Yasemin."* I didn't want to ask her anything else. I was hesitant to say something that would bother her parents who were sitting quietly on the sofa bed. After all, she was a child, she wouldn't know the problems adults were saddled with. She had no idea she wasn't supposed to talk about these problems.

I wasn't exactly wondering why this family I had traveled here with from Istanbul in the same minibus wanted to pass into Greece. I didn't understand what they were fleeing from. They were both Turks. Who knows what stories they had? While pondering what sort of story her parents had, Yasemin's curiosity knew no bounds. Her eyes were planting on my star tattoo on my chin. Finally, she couldn't resist and touching my chin with her tiny pointer finger, asked me, *"What's this?"* I replied, *"That's my star."* Yasemin's queries kept coming. Her last question was *"Why did you want it?"* My last answer was *"I wanted it to remind me I needed to be strong every time I looked in the mirror."*

Yes, I had this star tattoo etched onto my chin so it would

remind me I had to be strong. Actually, I intended to have a tattoo on my face that resembled those of Anita. Yusuf was aware of this and he was totally stunned when I told him I wanted to have a tattoo done on my chin. Before leaving Istanbul, when I told Yusuf I wanted to have a star tattoo done up, he asked me, *"Weren't you going to have one of Anita's tattoos made?"* When in fact, I also told Anita the day I met her that I would wait until I got my life in order to get an Inuit tattoo. Yusuf had also heard me say this. So, as I was still in the middle of my ordeal, I had to emerge victorious in every battle I took on, and if not, I still had to come out alive and kicking. That's why I wanted to have a tattoo that reminded me to be strong.

I remembered Anita's words quite vividly, "Some tattoos remind us to get ourselves together at our most vulnerable moment." The tattoo that would remind me to be strong was none other than the star on my mother's chin. Etched into her chin for good fortune, the star tattoo didn't serve its purpose. It's for this reason it was going to be my finest reminder. I was going to recall the anguish my mother suffered as well as my own suffering whenever I looked at that star on my chin. I was going to continue on my way, saying, *"This much suffering didn't beat us yet and that in the future isn't going to beat us either."* As Anita put it, *"What tattoos remind you only bring you a good fortune, not their mystical power. You create your own fortune."*

My star had another meaning hiding in the depths, but I didn't tell Yasemin that one. Actually, my star was Yusuf. When we came out of the tattoo parlor in Taksim, he held my hand and said, *"You know, you're supposed to remember you need to be strong whenever you look at your star, you can remember me too, Hifza."* I looked in his eyes and replied, *"I will never forget you. I will not have to remember you. Just as I've got this star on my face, I've got you in my heart."* If only we were able to be together a little longer. We loved each other quickly and we separated even quicker.

While praying I could stay on my feet on our final journey, and see Yusuf once more, I answered Yasemin's question, *"What's your name?"* I said, *"Hifza,"* saying it syllable by syllable. She still couldn't pronounce it right. She could only say *"Hida"* with her childlike pronunciation. I liked that a lot, being renamed by a child was as exciting as being reborn. I grinned as Yasemin repeated my name. Meanwhile, her mother said from the other side of the room, *"Sweetheart, leave her alone, let her rest. C'mon over here."* But Yasemin had no intention of leaving my side. Yasemin replied coyly, *"Mommy, I'm going to sit next to Hida."* That's when her mother got up and slowly came over to us.

She was going to take Yasemin and turn around, but my sudden question halted her. *"Don't you misunderstand me, but why are you running away? I mean, there's no war, no starvation, no fear of death in Turkey. Besides, you don't look like the type to be running away."* I asked. She had Yasemin's hand and replied me in a whisper, *"Yes there is no fear of death, but my husband committed a big crime and there is the fear of thrown in prison. At least for us."* I continued speaking excitedly while my mother's namesake sat back down on the sofa bed next to her husband. I exclaimed, *"You know something, there's a Turk at the camp in Greece who is assisting my brother."* Yasemin's father, who had kept silent until that moment, sat up and asked, *"Really, I wonder who that can be, do you know?"* I said that I didn't know, but he was someone who put us in contact with my brother. Yasemin's father had the intention of talking, asking what the Turk was doing in the camp and how he was helping out. So, I gave them a short rundown of the start of our story and delved in the part about my brother Ahmed.

As far as I could tell, Yasemin's father was trying to figure out who the Turk was at the camp. I inserted all the information my brother said about that Turk and told Yasemin's father the following; *"My brother thought we were in Syria when he entered the camp. He found a phone from one of his fellow refugees in his room and tried calling our relatives in Syria but couldn't reach anyone. As it was, we had no cellphones ourselves. One day, a Turk came into the room he was staying in. He was tall, spoke English and Arabic well, said he was from Ankara, and cared for my brother. Once my brother told him what had happened to him, he said, **'The area where you lived was under attack. If your family's alive, they've most likely passed into Turkey.'** When my brother told him that my mother was already a Turkish citizen and that she had relatives on her mother's side in Viransehir, the Turk took out his phone from his pocket and handed it to my brother. My brother didn't know the name of even one of our relatives, let alone their telephone numbers. But the Turk didn't give up as he took his phone back and found the number of the census bureau online. He made the call himself as my brother's Turkish wasn't very good. They hung up on them every time they called. Finally, a civil servant dealt with my brother once he heard mother's name. He gave him the number of my uncle in Istanbul. Then they called my uncle. We were also in Istanbul at the time when my uncle came and found us. You already know the rest."*

Then I thought about the official who gave my brother my uncle's number. He was none other than Kemal Ergin, who gave us the last money in his pocket so we could get to Istanbul. Kemal Ergin, who didn't use after we left Viransehir, who tried finding my mother's relatives, who set aside my uncle Bahattin's number, saying it might be necessary. Kemal Ergin, who gave my brother my uncle's number and the address we were at as he heard my mother's name. I'm never going to forget his name and what he did for us. If only I had his e-mail address so I could write him a thank you letter before passing over to Greece.

It was possible now, but I'm most definitely going to go to Viransehir and thank him one day. If I come back one day, I'm going to thank Mother Leyla and aunt Meryem and her children. In fact, I'm going to thank the host of this home where we spent our final night before passing over to Greece for letting me use his computer. Before I die, I'm going to thank all the good people whom I encounter. After all, none of us will emerge alive from the life we live. We're going to wear out, get injured and in the end, die. However, thanks to the good people we encounter, we're going to die without suffering or else with the least suffering.

Anita Tagaq
"Damn it, there's just too much agony."
October 4th, 2014
Toronto

I'**m very sorry.** I'm sorry I wasn't good for anything other than accumulating the painful memories of two youths. I'm sorry I was unable to help them. I'm so sorry that I'm ashamed of the breathing. I'm sorry to list dozens of 'if only's. If only I didn't go after the history of tattoos. If only I didn't travel to Turkey, if only I didn't meet Yusuf. If only I didn't see Hifza. If only I didn't get to know their mothers and listen to their stories. If only I didn' insist *"Keep a diary of everything that happens to you, even if it's brief."* If only I didn't collect their memoirs that Sevda had translated into English, *"So everyone can know."* Fine so I did these things, but if only I hadn't read that last e-mail Sevda sent. It was so obvious it had borne dreadful news. But how long could I have plugged my ears to this painful reality, even if it happened on the other side of the globe.

With every email she'd send me, Sevda would add comments of a few words that constituted different feelings in the subject heading. This time, she left the subject heading vacant. There wasn't even an emoji that smiled, cried, that was surprised or was disgusted. At the first moment, I thought Sevda would be fed up with translating. But no, such a thing wasn't possible. That's because she told me plenty of times that she enjoyed doing these translations. She told me time in and time our that she earned money from the work she did at the translation office she worked out and earned life experience from the stories of Yusuf and Hifza. She would go into detail about the things that happened to Yusuf and Hifza during our phone conversations. Sometimes she was furious, most of the time, she was sad. Sometimes she commented on the experiences of the two young people with LOL. She couldn't keep laughing especially when she talked about the exploits that occured in the pickle shop. Then again, she was saying, *"I'm really concerned about these kids"* in all of our conversations. She was right to be worried. Yusuf, and especially Hifza's lives, were no different from that of pigeons trying to fly against the reverse wind in order to escape predators. It was hazardous to try to fly but landing on the ground was even more hazardous. Was the pigeon shot while flying, or was it exhausted and become prey for hunters when it alighted? There was no way of knowing without reading her email.

Actually, I always preserved my hope after reading the translation of the e-mail Hifza sent to Sevda from her final stop on her trip to Greece. Hifza and her mother were going to pass over to Greece, reunite with Ahmed and become a family again even though they didn't have their father. What's that, it didn't happen? Where they caught by the border guards without crossing the river, did something happen to their boat, or else was I having visions? Maybe there was also good news in the email. I ticked on the e-mail line with the hope of receiving some good news. It was the translation of Yusuf's e-mail facing me. It started off with, *"I want to die."* I couldn't read the rest of the text. I got up from my table, went into the kitchen and made myself a strong, black cup of coffee. I took a sip of my coffee, which was as heady as I liked it. I steadied myself in order to read the rest of the email. I felt like I was a doctor who was evaluating the blood test tube of a kid threatened with leukemia. Even though I didn't want to learn the truth, I was obliged to read that text. I needed to add it to previous memories, good or bad, regardless of what was written.

I took the seat at the table to read the text. The monitor of my notebook darkened as I hadn't used it for a long time. My heart dropped as I moved the mouse. The monitor brightened. Once again, the first thing that struck my eyes was Yusuf's words, *"I want to die."* I took another sip of my coffee and continued reading. Yusuf's sentences were getting more and more heavier. Normally I'd make correct the incoming texts and add them to the memoir pages. I couldn't touch any of Yusuf's words even if they were translated. I copied the text in its original state and stuck them to the memoirs file. Yusuf's final letter consisted of two paragraphs:

"After they left Istanbul, we hadn't heard from Hifza and her mother for four days. It rained so heavily the day after they left Istanbul, the Meric River flooded the villages along its banks. Our fears increased the more we watched the flood images on the TV news. We called the Afghan refugee and reached Ahmed. He said that nobody had arrived yet and that he was waiting to hear from us. We raised our hopes when he said **'Maybe they were detained at the border guard station.'** *But*

news never came our way. As a last resort, we called Hifza's uncle Bahattin to the house. We wanted him to contact the smugglers and ask them what situation Hifza and her mother were in. He grumbled, but he called the smugglers. After first, the smugglers didn't answer their phone. When we persisted with our calling, someone picked up the phone. **'They got in the boat and left the bank, the rest was up to them, we don't now. But there was a lot of rainfall. I hope they were able to get to the other side'** *he said. I sensed there were something fishy about the situation when the smuggler wanted to hang up the phone as soon as possible.*

We waited all the way until the evening news. When the commentator said, **'Now we're linking into Edirne to get the latest developments regarding the flood disaster'** *I was worried to death. The bald correspondent who was wearing a macintosh and rainboots, spoke quickly into a microphone in one hand and a notebook in the other. Following clichéd intro sentences, he said,* **'During the morning hours, search and rescue teams reached a woman's body on the bank of the Meric. Two other women's bodies were found in the same region in the afternoon.'** *I was creeped out when the correspondent continued by saying,* **'It was determined that one of the bodies belongs to a teacher named Zehra Alaca, the wife of a police commissioner who has a warrant for his arrest.'** *I shouted,* **'My Allah, please say the other two women are this woman's relatives.'** *My mother tried to soothe me, saying,* **'Son, why say such a thing, does one feel relieved with someone else's pain? Take shelter in Allah, calm down.'** *I knew the words I said were cruel, but I couldn't accept the possibility that Hifza could be dead. But I knew I had nothing left to think about when the correspondent declared,* **'Officials believe the two women were Syrians with star tattoos on their faces who drowned while trying to pass over to**

Greece.' *I didn't die of anxiety, but now I could die of sorrow."*

Yusuf began his email by saying *"I want to die,"* ended it again by saying, *"I want to die."* What was I supposed to do with these memoir pages now? When in fact, I had wanted to collect these painful memories so these two young people could read on their happy days. These pages were nothing but a requiem registry for me now. I was crushed as I burst into tears. I took my dog Mocca and went outside to get some fresh air and relax. I walked in the park that had a creek flowing down the middle. I thought of Hifza's ordeal in the rushing river while I walked along the bank of the creek. I imagined how she thrashed about until her strength was depleted. I heard the screams of her mother and the other woman.

I was experiencing a nightmare. It was so huge that I found myself at the other end of the park in which I'd never walked to the end before. It was about to get dark outside. Turning back, I thought what would happen if Mocca fell into that creek. Of course, I'd jump in right after her and rescue my best buddy, my beautiful girl. What if there wasn't the possibility of saving her, if it was too dark, or if the water was too deep? I would've been overwhelmed. In fact, I was overwhelmed just thinking about that. I suddenly hugged Mocca's neck as she was walked in front of me. I let her get saucy and jump on me, lick my face. I petted her soft brown fur. I was smack dab in the midst of one of the contradictions that Hifza experienced. The person who is overwhelmed by the possibility of her dog falling into the stream has a heart, as does those who drag desperate people behind them to drown in the river.

I cried as I returned home. Mocca was happy, and I was in abject sorrow. I made myself another coffee. I didn't drink any wine, even though I really wanted to do so. I knew that if I drank in such moments, that I wouldn't be able to let go of the wine glass until I got totally smashed. I kind of wanted to write some things beneath Yusuf's letter while I was sober. I might drink some wine later on, try to forget what I read and diminish the flame that burned my heart. I didn't shut down my computer as I went out of the house. I moved the mouse around as the monitor went bright, and the memoir pages were facing me. I read Yusuf's letter once more. I jotted down a few sentences below the text.

Three women drowned in a river. A young man was embittered in İstanbul. Why? The answer to that is hidden in Hifza and Yusuf's agonizing experiences which occurred in their youth. In the end, power and financial ambition feeds hypocrisy, hypocrisy feeds evil, and evil feeds death. I hope that the little sandy haired girl, Yasemin and her father Hifza had mentioned, managed to survive this dreadfully vicious circle.

Damn it, there's just too much agony.

I will have a star tattoo on my chin.